L. MARIE ADELINE

S·E·C·R·E·T

A Novel

BROADWAY PAPERBACKS
NEW YORK

BROADWAY

Copyright © 2013 by L. Marie Adeline

Published in the United States by Broadway Paperbacks, an imprint of the
Crown Publishing Group, a division of Random House, Inc., New York.

www.crownpublishing.com

Broadway Paperbacks and its logo, a letter B bisected on the diagonal, are
trademarks of Random House, Inc.

Simultaneously published in Canada by Doubleday Canada, a division of
Random House of Canada Limited, Toronto.

Library of Congress Cataloging-in-Publication Data
is available upon request.

ISBN 978-0-385-34643-6
EISBN 978-0-385-34644-3

Printed in the United States of America

Book design by CS Richardson
Cover design by Jim Massey
Cover photography by Peter Locke

10 9 8 7 6 5 4 3 2 1

First Edition

To Nita

Waitresses are adept at reading body language. So are wives who've lived under the same roof as angry drunks. And I had been both, a wife for fourteen years and a waitress for almost four. Part of my job was to know, sometimes even before customers did, what they wanted. I could do that with my ex, too, anticipate exactly what he wanted the second he came through the door. And yet whenever I tried to turn that skill on myself, to anticipate my own needs, I couldn't.

I hadn't planned to become a waitress. Does anyone? I got the job at Café Rose after my ex died. And in the following four years, as I moved from grief to anger to a kind of numb limbo, I waited. I waited on people, I waited on time, I waited on life. Still, I actually kind of liked my job. Working in a place like Café Rose, in a city like New Orleans, you get your regulars, your favorites and a few you try to pawn off on your co-workers. Dell couldn't stand serving the local eccentrics because they were bad tippers.

But I overheard the best stories. So we had a trade-off. I would take the eccentrics and the musicians if she waited on the students, or anyone with babies and strollers.

My absolute favorites were the couples, this one couple in particular. Strange maybe to say this, but I'd get butter-flies whenever they walked in. The woman was in her late thirties, beautiful in the way some French women are—glowing skin, short hair, and yet she had an undeniably feminine air. Her man, the guy she always came in with, had an open face, with brown hair shaved close to his head. He was tall with a lean, lithe body, and a little younger than her, I think. Neither the man nor the woman wore wedding rings, so I wasn't sure about the exact nature of their rela-tionship. But whatever it was, it was intimate. They always looked like they'd just come from having sex or were head-ing to do just that after a quick lunch.

Every time they sat down, they did this thing where the guy would place his elbows on the table, opening up his hands to face her. She'd wait a beat, then gently place her elbows on the table in front of his, and they'd suspend their hands, palms open, an inch from each other's, as though there was a gentle force preventing them from touching—just for a second, before it got cheesy or was noticeable to anyone but me. Then their fingers would interlock. He would kiss the tips of her fingers, now framed by the backs of his hands, one after the other. Always left to right. She would smile. All this happened quickly, so quickly, before they'd separate their hands and scan the menu. Watching them, or trying to watch without seeming to watch, triggered a deep, familiar longing in me. I could feel what she felt, as though it was his hand caressing mine, or my forearm, my wrist.

The life I'd lived held no such longings. Tenderness wasn't familiar to me. Nor urgency. My ex-husband, Scott, could be kind and generous when he was sober, but towards the end, when his drinking had him by the throat, he was anything but. After he died, I cried for all the pain he had been in and all the pain he had caused, but I didn't miss him. Not even a little. Something atrophied in me, then died, and soon five years had passed since I'd had sex. Five Years. I often thought of this accidental celibacy like it was a skinny old dog, left with no choice but to follow me. Five Years came with me everywhere, tongue lolling, trotting on its toes. When I tried on clothes, Five Years lay panting on the floor of the change room, its gleaming eyes ridiculing my attempt to look prettier in a new dress. Five Years also parked itself beneath every table of every tepid date I went on, slumped at my feet.

None of the dates I'd been on had led me to a relationship of any value. At thirty-five, I'd begun to believe "it" would never happen again. To be wanted, to be craved, the way this man craved this woman, was like something out of a foreign movie in a language I'd never learn, with subtitles that were becoming increasingly blurry.

"Third date," my boss mumbled, startling me. I was standing next to Will behind the pastry counter, where he was wiping dishwasher spots off the glasses. He had noticed me noticing the couple. And I noticed his arms as I always did. He was wearing a plaid shirt, rolled to the elbows, his forearms muscular and covered with soft sun-bleached hair. Though we were just friends, every once in a while I was a little shaken by his sexiness, enhanced by the fact that he was completely oblivious to it.

"Maybe fifth date, don't you think? Is that how long women wait before they sleep with a guy they're dating?"

"I wouldn't know."

Will rolled his dark blue eyes at me. He no longer tolerated my whining about my lack of dates.

"Those two were like that from day one," I said, glancing back at my couple. "They're totally into each other."

"I give them six months," Will said.

"Cynic," I replied, shaking my head.

We often did this, speculated on the imaginary relationship between two customers. It was our little thing, a way to pass the time.

"Okay, look over there. See that old guy splitting a plate of mussels with that young woman?" he said, pointing out a different couple, discreetly, with his chin. I craned my neck, trying not to stare too obviously at an older man with a much younger woman.

"I bet that's his best friend's daughter," Will said, lowering his voice. "She's finally graduated and wants to apprentice at his law office. But now that she's twenty-one, he's going to put the moves on her."

"Ew. What if she's just his daughter?"

Will shrugged.

I scanned the room, surprisingly busy for a Tuesday afternoon. I pointed out yet another couple, in the corner just finishing their meal. "Now, see those two?"

"Yeah."

"I think they're just about to break up," I said. Will gave me a look like I was going too far into fantasyland. "There's almost no eye contact at all between them, and he was the only one to order a dessert. I brought him two spoons, but he didn't even offer her a bite. Bad sign."

"Always a bad sign. A man should *always* share his dessert," he said, winking. I had to smile. "Hey, can you finish polishing the glasses? I have to pick up Tracina. Her car broke down again."

Tracina was the night waitress Will had been dating for a little over a year, after asking me out didn't get him anywhere. I was initially flattered by his interest in me, but I was in no position to act on it. I needed a friend more than I needed to be dating my boss. Plus, we eventually crossed so deep into the friend zone that despite my attraction, it was less of a struggle to keep things platonic . . . except for the odd time that I'd catch him working late in the back office, the top button of his shirt undone, his sleeves rolled up, running his fingers through his thick, salt-and-pepper hair. But I could shake the feeling off.

Then he started dating Tracina. I once accused him of hiring her just so he could take her out.

"So what if I did? It's one of the few perks of being the boss," he said.

After I finished polishing the glasses, I printed up my couple's bill and made my way slowly to their table. That's when I noticed the woman's bracelet for the first time, a thick gold chain festooned with small gold charms.

It was so unusual, a pale yellow with a matte finish. The charms had Roman numerals on them on one side and words, which I couldn't quite read, on the other. There were about a dozen charms on the chain. The man seemed captivated by this piece of jewelry, too. He ran his fingers through the charms as he caressed her wrist and forearm with both hands. His touch was firm, possessive in a way that caught me in the throat and caused the area behind my belly button to warm up. *Five Years.*

"Here you go," I said, my voice rising an octave. I slid the bill on the part of the table not covered by their limbs. They seemed astonished by my presence.

"Oh. Thanks!" the woman said, straightening.

"Was everything okay?" I asked. Why was I feeling shy towards them?

"Perfect as always," she said.

"It was great, thanks," the man added, digging for his wallet.

"Let me get this one. You always pay." The woman leaned sideways and pulled her wallet from her purse and gave me a credit card. Her bracelet tinkled as she moved. "Here you go, sweetheart." She was my age and calling me "sweetheart"?

Her confidence let her get away with it. When I took the credit card, I thought I saw concern flash across her eyes. Was she noticing my stained brown work shirt? The one I always wore because it matched the color of the food that ended up on it? I felt suddenly aware of my appearance. I also realized I wasn't wearing any makeup. Oh God, and my shoes— brown and flat. No stockings—ankle socks, if you can believe it. What had happened to me? When had I turned prematurely into a middle-aged frump?

My face burned as I walked away, shoving the credit card in my apron. I headed straight for the washroom to splash cold water on my face. I smoothed down my apron and looked in the mirror. I wore brown clothing because it was practical. I can't wear a dress. I am a waitress. As for my messy ponytail, hair has to be tied back. It's regulation. I supposed I could comb it back more smoothly, instead of sloppily wrapping it up in an elastic like a clutch of aspara- gus. My shoes were the shoes of a woman who hadn't given a lot of thought to her feet, despite how nice I've been told mine are. And it's true that I hadn't had a professional mani- cure since the night before my wedding. But those things are a waste of money. Still, how had I let it come to this? I had officially let myself go. Five Years lay slumped against the bathroom door, exhausted. I returned to the table with the credit card slip, avoiding eye contact with either of them.

"Have you worked here long?" the man asked, while the woman scribbled her signature.

"About four years."

"You're very good at your job."

"Thank you." I felt heat rise in my face.

"We'll see you next week," the woman said. "I just love this old place."

"It's seen better days."

"It's perfect for us," she added, handing me the bill and winking at her man.

I looked at her signature, expecting something florid and interesting. *Pauline Davis* seemed plain and small, which was kind of reassuring to me in that moment.

My eyes followed the couple as they left, walking past the tables and outside, where they kissed and parted ways. As she passed the front window, the woman glanced in at me and waved. I must have looked like such a dork, standing there staring at them. I waved meekly back at her through the dusty glass.

My trance was broken by an elderly woman sitting at the next table. "That lady dropped something," she said, pointing under the table.

I bent to retrieve a small, burgundy notebook. It looked well worn and was soft to the touch, like skin. The cover had the initials *PD* embossed in gold, the same gold edging the pages. I gingerly opened it to the first page, looking for Pauline's address or number, and accidentally caught a glimpse of the contents: *". . . his mouth on me . . . never felt so alive . . . it shot through me like a white-hot . . . coming over me in waves, swirling . . . bent me over the . . ."*

I slapped the diary shut.

"You might be able to catch her," said the woman, slowly chewing a pastry. I noticed she was missing a front tooth.

"Probably too late," I said. "I'll . . . just hold on to it. She's in here a lot."

The woman shrugged and pulled another strip off her croissant. I tucked the notebook into my waitressing pouch, a shiver of excitement running up my spine. For the rest of my shift, until Tracina arrived in her impatient bubble-gum haze, spiral curls bouncing in her high ponytail, the note-book felt alive in my front pocket. For the first time in a long time, New Orleans at dusk didn't seem quite as lonely.

On my walk home, I counted the years. It had been six since Scott and I first came to New Orleans from Detroit to start over. Housing was cheap and Scott had just lost the last job he ever hoped to hold in the auto industry. We both thought a fresh start in a new city looking to rebuild itself after a hurricane would be a good backdrop for a marriage hoping to do the same thing.

We found a cute little blue house on Dauphine Street, in Marigny, where other young people were flocking. I had some luck finding a job as a vet's assistant at an animal shelter in Metairie. But Scott blew through several positions on the rigs and then he blew two years of sobriety when a night of drinking turned into a two-week bender. After he hit me for the second time in two years, I knew it was over. I suddenly got the sense of how much effort it had taken him to hold off hitting me since the first time he'd taken a drunken fist to my face. I moved a few blocks away to a one-bedroom apartment, the first and only place I looked at.

One night a few months later, Scott called to see if I'd meet him at Café Rose so he could make amends for his behavior, and I agreed. He'd stopped drinking, he said, this time for good. But his apologies sounded hollow and his demeanor still flinty and defensive. By the end of our meal I was fighting back tears and he was standing over me hissing a final few *sorry*s over my lowered head.

"I *do* mean it. I know I don't sound sorry, but in my heart, Cassie, I live every day with what I did to you. I don't know how to make you get over it," he said, and then he stormed out.

Of course he left me with the bill.

On my way out, I noticed the job posting for a lunch waitress. I had long been thinking about quitting my job at the vet clinic. There I took care of the cats and walked the dogs on the afternoon shift, but the post-Katrina strays weren't getting adopted, so my job mostly consisted of shaving spots on the skinny legs of otherwise healthy animals in preparation for euthanasia. I began to hate going to work every day. I hated looking into those sad, tired eyes. That night I filled out an application for the restaurant.

That was also the night the road washed out near Parlange, and Scott drove his car into False River and drowned.

I did wonder whether it was an accident or a suicide, but fortunately our insurance company didn't question it—he was sober, after all. And since the guardrails had rusted at the bolts, I received a healthy settlement from the county. But what was Scott doing out there that night anyway? It was so like him to make a grandiose exit that would leave me laden with guilt. I wasn't happy to see him dead. But I wasn't sad either. And it was there, in that numb limbo, that I had remained ever since.

Two days after flying back from his funeral in Ann Arbor—where I sat alone because Scott's family blamed me for his death—I got a phone call from Will. At first, his voice kind of threw me, its timbre so much like Scott's, minus the slurring.

"Am I speaking with Cassie Robichaud?"

"You are. Who's this?"

"My name's Will Foret. I own Café Rose? You dropped off a résumé last week. We're looking for someone to start right away for the breakfast and lunch shift. I know you don't have a lot of experience, but I got a good vibe from you when we met the other day, and—"

A good vibe?

"When did we meet?"

"When you, uh, dropped off your résumé."

"I'm sorry, of course I remember. Sorry, yes, I could come in on Thursday."

"Thursday's good. How about ten-thirty. I'll show you the ropes."

Forty-eight hours later, I was shaking Will's hand, and shaking my head at the fact that I actually hadn't remembered him—that's how out of it I'd been that night. We joke about it now ("Yeah, the time I completely bowled you over with my first impression, *that you don't even remember!*"), but I was in such a fog after that fight with Scott that I could have spoken with Brad Pitt and failed to notice. So meeting Will again, I was taken aback at how unassumingly handsome he was.

Will didn't promise I'd make great money; the Café is just a bit north of the hot spots, and isn't open at night. He mentioned something about expanding upstairs, but that was years away.

"Mostly locals hang out and eat here. Tim and the guys from Michael's bike shop. Lotta musicians. Some you'll find sleeping in the doorway because they've played on the stoop all night. Local characters who like to linger for hours. But they all drink a lot of coffee."

"Sounds good."

His job training consisted of an unenthusiastic tour where he pointed and mumbled instructions on how to use the dishwasher and the coffee grinder and where he kept the cleaning supplies.

"City says you have to wear your hair tied back. Other than that, I'm not too picky. We don't have uniforms, but it's a fast turnaround at lunch, so be practical."

"'Practical' is my middle name," I said.

"I do plan to renovate," he said, when he saw me noticing a chip in the tile floor and, later, a wobbly ceiling fan. The place was run-down but homey and only a ten-minute walk from my apartment at Chartres and Mandeville. He told me he named it Café Rose after Rose Nicaud, an ex-slave who used to sell her own blend of coffee from a cart on the streets of New Orleans. Will was distantly related to her on his mother's side, he said.

"You should see our family reunion pictures. It's like a group shot from the United Nations. Every color represented . . . So? You want the job?"

I nodded enthusiastically, and Will shook my hand again.

After that, my life shrunk to a few essential blocks of Marigny. Maybe I'd go to Tremé to hear Angela Rejean, one of Tracina's friends who worked at Maison. Or I'd wander antique or second-hand shops on Magazine. But I rarely went beyond those neighborhoods, and stopped going to the Museum of Art or Audubon Park altogether. In fact, it may be strange to say, but I could have gone the rest of my life in the city without ever seeing the water.

I did mourn. After all, Scott was the first and only man I'd ever been with. I'd break down crying at odd times, while on a bus or in the middle of brushing my teeth. Waking from a long nap in a darkened bedroom always triggered tears. But it wasn't just Scott I mourned. I mourned the loss of nearly fifteen years of my life spent listening to his constant put-downs and complaints. And that's what I was left with. I didn't know how to shut off the critical voice that, in Scott's absence, continued to note my flaws and highlight my mistakes. *How come you haven't joined a gym? No one wants a woman over thirty-five. All you do is watch TV. You could be so much prettier if you just made an effort.* Five Years.

I threw myself into work. The pace suited me well. We served the only breakfast on the street, nothing fancy: eggs any way, sausage, toast, fruit, yogurt, pastries and croissants. Lunch was never elaborate: soups and sandwiches, or sometimes a one-pot dish like bouillabaisse, lentil stew or a jambalaya if Dell came in early and felt like whipping something up. She was a better cook than a waitress, but she couldn't stand being in the kitchen all day.

I only worked four days a week, from nine to four, sometimes later if I stuck around for a meal and a visit with Will. If Tracina was running late, I'd start her tables for her. I never complained. I always kept busy.

I could have made more money in the afternoons, but I liked the morning shift. I loved hosing the night's dirt off the grimy sidewalk first thing in the morning. I loved how the sun freckled the patio tables. I loved stocking the pastry display case, while the coffee brewed and the soup simmered. I loved taking my time to cash out, spreading my money on one of the tippy tables by the big front windows. But there was always something lonely about heading home.

My life began to take on a steady, reliable rhythm: work, home, read, sleep. Work, home, read, sleep. Work, *movie*, home, read, sleep. It wouldn't have taken a superhuman effort to shift out of it, but I just couldn't make a change.

I thought that after a while I would automatically start living again, dating even. I thought there'd be a magical day when the rut would fill itself in, and I'd join the world again. Like a switch would turn on. The idea of taking a course crossed my mind. Finishing my degree. But I was too numb to commit. I was slouching towards middle age with no brakes on, my fat calico cat, Dixie, a former stray, aging right along with me.

"You say you have a fat cat like it's something that *she* caused," Scott used to say to me. "She didn't get here fat. You did this to her."

Scott didn't give in to Dixie and her constant whining for food. Me, however, she worked over until I caved, again and again. I had no resolve, which is probably why I put up with Scott for so long. It took me a while to realize that I didn't cause his drinking, nor could I stop it, but there was this lingering sense that I might have saved him if I had tried hard enough.

Maybe if we had had a baby like he wanted. I never told him how secretly relieved I was to learn that I couldn't have kids. Surrogacy was an option, but it was too expensive to be a viable one for us, and thankfully Scott wasn't keen on adoption. That I never wanted to be a mother was never in dispute. But I still hoped for a sense of purpose in life, for something to take up that space that a yearning for children had never occupied.

⟽⟾

A few months after I started working at the Café, and way before Tracina stole his heart, Will hinted that he could get tickets for a coveted show at the jazz festival. At first, I thought he was going to tell me about a girlfriend he was getting the tickets for, but as it turned out, it was me he wanted to go with. I felt a flash of panic at the invitation.

"So . . . you're asking if I'll go out with you?"

"Uh . . . yes." There was that look again, and for a second I thought I even saw hurt flicker through his eyes. "Front row, Cassie. Come on. It's a good excuse to put on a dress. I've never seen you in a dress, come to think of it."

I knew then that I had to shut it down. I couldn't date. I couldn't date *him*. My *boss*. There was no way I wanted to lose a job I actually liked for a man who would, when he spent a bit of time with me, see just how dull I really was. Also, the man was way out of my league. I was paralyzed with fear and the prospect of being alone with him, outside the context of our working relationship.

"You haven't seen me in a dress because I don't own one," I said.

Not true. I just couldn't imagine putting one on. Will was quiet for a few seconds, wiping his hands on his apron.

"No big deal," he said. "Lots of people want to see this band."

"Will, look. I think being married to such a wreck for so many years might have rendered me kind of . . . undatable," I said, sounding like a late-night radio psychologist.

"That's a nice way of saying, 'It's not you, it's me.'"

"But it *is* me. It is."

I rested my hand on his forearm.

"I guess I'll just ask the next attractive girl I hire," he joked.

And he did. He asked the stunning Tracina from Texarkana, with the Southern accent and the endless legs. She had a younger brother with autism who she fiercely cared for, and she owned more cowboy boots than any one person needs. She was hired for the early evening shift, and though she was always a little cool towards me, we got along well enough and she seemed to make Will happy. Saying good-night to him became doubly lonely because I knew he'd probably be spending the night at Tracina's instead of upstairs at the Café. Not that I was jealous. How could I be jealous? Tracina was exactly the kind of girl Will should be with—funny, smart and sexy. She had perfect cocoa-colored skin. Sometimes she'd let her afro go wild like a mound of cotton candy, and sometimes she'd expertly tame it into cool braids. Tracina was sought after. Tracina was vivacious. Tracina fit in and belonged. I simply did not.

That night, the notebook still warming my front pocket, I watched Tracina set up for the dinner crowd. It was the first time I admitted I actually was a little jealous of her. Not because she had Will. I was jealous of how she made her way around the room with such ease and appeal. Some women had that thing, that ability to insert themselves directly into life—and look so good doing it. They weren't observers; they were in the middle of the action. They were . . . alive. Will asked her out and she said, "I'd love to." No dithering, no equivocating, just a big fat yes.

I thought about the notebook, the words I had scanned, that man at the table, the way he caressed his partner's wrist and kissed her fingers. How he fingered her bracelet, his urgency. I wished some man could feel that for me. I thought of a fistful of thick hair in my hands, my back pressed against a wall in the kitchen of the restaurant, a hand lifting my skirt. Wait a second, the man with Pauline had a shaved head. I was imagining Will's hair, Will's mouth . . .

"A penny for your thoughts," Will said, interrupting my absurd daydream.

"These ones are worth a lot more than a penny," I said, knowing my face was shot red. Where had that come from? My shift was over. It was time to go.

"Good tips today?"

"Yeah, not bad. I gotta run, and, Will, I don't care if you *are* sleeping with her. Tell Tracina to restock sugar on the table before she goes home tonight. They should be full for my breakfast shift."

"Yes, boss," he said, saluting me. Then, as I was heading out the door, he added, "Plans tonight?"

Catching up on TV. Recycling is piling up. What else?

"Yeah, big plans," I said.

"You should have a date with a man, not with a cat, Cassie. You're a lovely woman, you know."

"*Lovely?* You didn't just call me 'lovely.' Will, that's what guys say to women over thirty-five who haven't gone completely to pot but who are well on their way to romantic retirement. '*You're a lovely woman, but . . .*'"

"But nothing. Cassie, you should get out there," he said, jerking his chin towards the front door and beyond.

"That's precisely where I'm headed," I said, backing into the street and nearly getting sideswiped by a speeding cyclist.

"Cassie! Jeez!" Will lurched towards me.

"See? That's what happens when I put myself out there. I get flattened," I said, calming my heart and trying to laugh it off.

Will shook his head as I turned and made my way down Frenchmen. I thought I felt him standing there watching me walk away, but I was too shy to turn around and check.

II

s it possible to feel really young and really old at the same
time? I was bone weary as I trudged the four blocks home.
I loved looking at the tired, tiny houses in my neighborhood, some leaning on each other, some coated with so
many layers of paint, and ringed by so much wrought iron
and festooned with so many ornate shutters that they
looked like aging showgirls in costumes and stage makeup.
My apartment was atop a three-story stucco block of a
house on the corner of Chartres and Mandeville. It was
painted pale green, with rounded arches and dark green
shutters. I had the top floor, but at thirty-five I still lived
like a student. My one-bedroom rental had a futon-couch,
milk carton bookshelves that doubled as end tables, and a
growing collection of salt-and-pepper shakers. The bedroom was in an alcove, with a wide stucco archway and
three dormers that faced south. To be fair, the staircase was
so narrow it prohibited big, fat furniture; everything had to
be portable and bendable and foldable. As I approached my

building and looked up, I realized I'd one day be too old to live on the top floor, especially if I continued to work on my feet. Some nights I was so tired, it was all I could do to heave myself up those stairs.

I had begun to note that as my neighbors got older, they didn't leave; they just moved to a lower floor. The Delmonte sisters had made the move a few months ago after Sally and Janette, two other sisters, finally moved to an assisted living facility. When the cozy two-bedroom was freed up, I helped them haul their books and clothes from the second to the first floor. There was a ten-year age difference between Anna and Bettina, and though Anna, at sixty, certainly could have taken the stairs for a few more years, Bettina forced her hand when she turned seventy. Anna was the one who told me that when the single-family dwelling was converted into five apartments in the '60s, it became known as the Spinster Hotel.

"It's always been all women," she said. "Not that *you're* a spinster, my dear. I know single women of a certain age are very sensitive to that word these days. Not that there's anything wrong with *being* a spinster, even if you *were* a spinster. Which you most certainly are *not*."

"I am a widow, though."

"Yes, but you're a *young* widow. Lots of time to remarry and have children. Well, to remarry at least," Anna said, one eyebrow up.

She slid me a dollar bill for my troubles, a gesture I had stopped resisting long ago as that bill would inevitably end up folded over eight times and shoved under my door a few hours later.

"You're a treasure, Cassie."

Was I a spinster? I had gone on one date last year, with Will's younger brother's best friend, Vince, a lanky hipster who gasped when I told him I was thirty-four. Then, to cover his shock, he leaned across the table and told me that he had a "thing" for older women—this from someone the ripe old age of thirty. I should have slapped his stupid face. Instead, an hour into our date I began glancing at my watch. He was talking too much about the crappy band that was playing and how bad the wine list was and how many run-down houses he was going to buy in New Orleans because the market was surely going to correct itself anytime now. When he dropped me off in front of the Spinster Hotel, I thought about asking him up. I thought about Five Years hunched in the back seat. *Just have sex with this guy, Cassie. What's stopping you? What's always stopped you?* But when I caught him spitting his gum out the window, I decided I just couldn't take off my clothes in front of this overgrown boy.

So much for my last date, I thought, as I prepped a bath and stripped off my waitress clothes. I wanted to wash the restaurant smell off me. I glanced down the hallway at the little notebook on the table by the front door. What was I supposed to do with it? Part of me knew I shouldn't read it, and the other was powerless to resist. So all through my shift I kept putting it off, thinking, *When you get home. After dinner. After a bath. When you get into bed. In the morning. Never?*

Dixie circled my ankles for food while water and bubbles filled the tub. The moon hovered over Chartres, and the sound of cicadas blotted out the traffic sounds. I looked in the mirror and tried to see myself as someone else would for the first time. It's not that my body was awful. It was a good body, not too tall, not too thin. I had dishpan hands, but overall I was in good shape, probably from waitressing all day. I liked the shape of my butt, it was nicely rounded— but it's true what they say about your late thirties: everything starts to soften. I held my C-cups in my hands and lifted them slightly. There. I imagined Scott, no, not Scott. Will, no, not him either. He was Tracina's, not mine. I imagined that guy, the one from the restaurant, coming up behind me and putting his hands on me like this, and bending me forward and then . . . *Stop it, Cassie.*

I had stopped getting those stupid Brazilian waxes after Scott died. The look always unsettled me, like I was supposed to be a little girl or something. I let my hand travel down to my . . . what? What do you call it when you're alone? *Vagina* always sounded by turns juvenile and clinical. *Pussy* was a guy's term and felt too feline for me. *Cunt?* No. Too much. I moved my finger around *down there*, and found, to my surprise, that I was wet. But I couldn't muster the energy, the effort, to do anything about it.

Was I lonely? Yes, of course. But I was also slowly shutting down parts of myself, seemingly for good, like a large factory going dark, sector by sector. I was only thirty-five and I had never had really great, mind-blowing, liberating, luscious sex, the kind that notebook seemed to allude to.

There were days when I felt I was just a suit of flesh pulled over a set of bones, pouring in and out of buses and cabs, walking around a restaurant, feeding people and cleaning up after them. At home, my body was a warm place for the cat to sleep on. How had this happened? How had this become my life? Why couldn't I just pick up the pieces and get out there, like Will had said?

I looked in the mirror again: all that flesh, all of it available and tender, yet somehow locked away. I stepped into the bath and sat down, then slid all the way under the water, submerging my head under the suds for a few seconds. I could hear my heart underwater, beating out a sad echo. That, I thought, is the sound of loneliness.

~

I rarely drank, let alone drank alone, but somehow that night called for a glass of cold white wine and a warm bathrobe. I had a box of Chablis in the fridge, albeit one that had been there for a couple of months, but it would have to do. I poured a big tumbler full. Then I settled into the corner of the futon-couch with the cat and the notebook. I traced the initials *PD* on the cover with my finger. Inside was a nameplate with *Pauline Davis* printed on it, but no contact information. That page was followed by a table of contents in scripted lettering, spelling out steps, one through ten:

Step One: Surrender
Step Two: Courage
Step Three: Trust
Step Four: Generosity
Step Five: Fearlessness
Step Six: Confidence
Step Seven: Curiosity
Step Eight: Bravery
Step Nine: Exuberance
Step Ten: The Choice

Oh my God, what did I have in my hands? What was this list? I felt hot and chilled at the same time, like I had uncovered a dangerous but delicious secret. I got up from the couch to draw down my lace curtains. *Fearlessness, Courage, Confidence, Exuberance?* These words had leapt out at me from the page, blurring before my eyes. Was Pauline taking these steps herself? And if so, where was she on the list? I sat down again and read the steps once more, then flipped the page to the next heading, "Fantasy Notes on Step One." I couldn't stop myself. I began to read:

I can't tell you how scared I was, how worried that I would chicken out, cancel, run. That's what I do, right? When things get overwhelming, esp. sexually. But I thought of the word

Acceptance, *and I became open to the idea that I should accept this, accept the help from S.E.C.R.E.T. But when he silently entered the hotel room and closed the door behind him, I knew I wanted to go through with it . . .*

I could feel my own heart beat as though *I* was in the hotel room as this stranger opened the door . . .

This guy! What can I say? Matilda was right. He was so damn sexy . . . he walked towards me slowly like a cat, and I backed away until the bed stopped me at the back of my knees. And then he sent me backwards on the bed with a gentle nudge, lifted my skirt and parted my legs. I pulled a pillow over my face after he uttered the only words he'd say that day: You are so fucking beautiful. And then he brought me into a kind of ecstasy I can't really describe here but I will try . . .

I shut the book again. It was wrong to read this. It was so raw. This was none of my business. I had to stop.

After one more Step. Then I'd stop. Then I would *most definitely* put this book away.

I opened it randomly to the middle, flashing forward, I assumed, through pages of sexy words:

Wow. First off, it was weird! I won't lie. But yet it had this incredible filling effect. That's the only way to describe it. Like I had it all inside me. Like I couldn't go any further and then I found I could. I didn't care how loud I was being. His hands were working me over all the while. It felt so incredible! Thank God the Mansion is soundproof, or so I'm told. It must be; otherwise everyone would know what was happening in each of these rooms. But I'll tell you, the best sensation came from the other guy, Olivier, who lay beneath me, my lovely dark-haired stranger with a full arm of tattoos, who was sucking on my . . .

I snapped the book closed. Okay, I had to stop. This was too much. Two men? At once? I looked to the top of the page. This was Step Five: *Fearlessness.* I was shocked that I felt damp between the legs. I didn't normally read erotic stuff, and when I came across pornography by accident, I rarely found it arousing. But this? This was all about *desire.* I wanted to read the whole thing, but no, I wouldn't. I held the book shut tight in my lap.

She didn't seem the type, Pauline, with her short hair and her clean looks. But what's "the type"? What's the furthest I'd ever gone with a man? The riskiest? A giggly handjob in a movie theater in high school with a boy I dated when Scott and I were on a "break." I'd given blowjobs. Maybe not well, and not always to completion. Sexually speaking, I was sorely inexperienced. Dixie had rolled onto her back in a posture that was appropriately lewd.

"Oh, kitty, you've probably had more fun in the streets than I've had in my bedroom."

I had to put the notebook away. To read any more of it would be to violate Pauline's privacy irrevocably, and to drive myself to distraction. I got up and almost angrily shoved the book deep into the drawer of the telephone table by my front door. After ten minutes, I moved it to a pocket of an old ski jacket I had brought from Michigan and left hanging in the back of the closet. Still, the book called for me. Then I put it in the broiler beneath the gas stove. But what if the pilot light ignited it?

I decided to put the notebook in my purse so I wouldn't forget to bring it to work the next day, in case Pauline came back to retrieve it. Oh God, what if she thinks I read it? But how could I not? Well, at least I didn't read all of it, I thought, taking the notebook out of my purse and finally locking it in the trunk of my car.

⟿

Two days later, after the lunch rush died down, the door chimes signaled the arrival of Pauline. My stomach lurched, like she was coming to arrest me. This time she wasn't with her sexy man but with a beautiful older woman, perhaps fifty or a well-preserved sixty with red wavy hair, wearing a pale coral tunic. They were both a little grim-faced as they made their way to an empty table by the window. I smoothed down my T-shirt and steeled myself as I approached the table. *Try not to look at her too long. Try to appear nonchalant, normal. You don't know anything because you never read the notebook.*

"Hi there. Start with coffee?" I asked, my lips pulled tight across my teeth, my heart bashing against my rib cage.

"Yes, please," said Pauline, avoiding eye contact with me and looking directly at the red-haired woman. "You?"

"I'll have green tea. And a couple of menus, please," she replied, staring back at Pauline.

I felt a rush of shame. They knew something. They knew *I* knew something.

"O-of course," I stammered, turning to the table.

"Wait. I was wondering . . ."

My heart leapt to my mouth.

"Yes?" I said, turning back, hands shoved deep in my front pouch, shoulders up at my ears.

It was Pauline who'd spoken. She was as nervous as I was. Her companion's face, however, was serene, supportive. I sensed a slight nod urging her on. I noticed the redhead also wore one of those beautiful gold bracelets, the same brushed pale finish and dangling charms.

"Did I forget something here the other day? A small booklet. About the size of this napkin. Burgundy. It has my initials on it, P. D. Did you find it?" Her voice was quivering. She looked on the verge of tears.

My eyes darted from hers to the calm face of her companion.

"Um. I don't know, but let me check with Dell," I said, way too brightly. "I'll be right back."

I walked stiffly back to the kitchen, punched the door open and stood with my back against the cool tile wall. All the air was gone from my lungs. I looked over at old Dell, who was cleaning the big pot that she'd used for the chili special. Though she kept her nearly white afro shorn close to her skull, she always wore a hairnet and a professional waitressing uniform. I had a lightning bolt of an idea.

"Dell! You have to do me a favor."

"I *have* to do no such thing, Cassie," she said with her slight lisp. "Use your manners."

"Okay. Really fast. These customers out there. One of them left something here, a small notebook, and I don't want her to think I read it. Because I did. I mean, not all of it. But I *had* to read some of it. How else would I know whose it was, right? But it was like a diary, and I might have read too much of it. And it was personal. Very. But I don't want them to know I read *any* of it. Can I say *you* found it? Please?"

"You want me to lie."

"No, no, I'll do *all* the lying."

"God, girl, sometimes I don't understand young women today with all your dramas and stories and such. You can't just say, '*Here, I found this*'?"

"Not this time, no. I can't."

I stood in front of Dell, hands clasped pleadingly.

"Fine," Dell said, waving me away like a fly. "So long as I don't have to say anything. Jesus didn't raise me to lie."

"I could kiss you."

"You could *not*," she said.

I ran to my locker, plucked the book from the top of a pile of dirty T-shirts and made a mental note to do laundry. I was breathless when I got to the table. The faces of both women turned towards me at the same time, expectant.

"So! I asked Dell. She's the other waitress who works days, too, right over there . . ." At this point, Dell dutifully came out of the kitchen and waved a tired arm our way to legitimize my total lie. "It turns out she found this," I said, triumphantly pulling the notebook out of my pouch. "Is this what you——?"

Before I could finish that sentence, Pauline plucked the book from my fingers and deposited it into her purse.

"That *is* it. And thank you so much," she said to me, exhaling. Then she turned to the other woman. "You know what? I have to go now, Matilda. So sad, but turns out I don't have time for lunch after all today, is that okay?"

"That's fine. Call me later. But *I'm* famished," Matilda said. She stood to hug her harried companion goodbye.

I could feel the relief and the vexation coursing through Pauline. She had gotten the booklet back, but she knew that it had released some of its secrets somewhere, to someone, and it seemed she couldn't wait to leave. After their quick embrace, she made a dash for the door.

Matilda folded back down into her chair, as relaxed as a cat settling into a sun patch. I looked around the restaurant. It was about three o'clock, and the place was almost empty. My shift would be over soon.

"Be right back with your green tea," I said. "Menu's on the wall there."

"Thank you, Cassie," she said as I walked away.

I felt gut-punched. She knew my name. How did she know my name? I did sign my bills. And Pauline was a regular. That's how. Surely.

The rest of my shift was uneventful. Matilda sipped her tea, looking out the window. She ordered the egg salad sandwich, pickle on the side, half of which she ate. We didn't say much beyond the pleasantries of a waitress serving a customer. I gave her the bill and she left a nice tip.

~~~

That's why I was shocked the next day to see Matilda come in after the lunch rush died down, this time alone. She waved at me and pointed to a table. I nodded, noticing that my hands shook a little as I made my way over to her. What I was so nervous about? Even if she knew I'd lied, what was so bad about what I had done? How could any normal person have resisted reading a notebook with such compelling content? Besides, it was Pauline who might feel wronged, her privacy a little violated, not this woman.

"Hello, Cassie," she said, smiling a genuine smile.

This time I noticed her face. She had bright wide eyes, dark brown, with flawless skin. She wore little makeup, which had the added effect of making her look younger than what she probably was, which I now suspected was closer to sixty than fifty. She had a heart-shaped face, which drew to an acute point at her chin, and she was, frankly, extraordinarily beautiful, in the way women with unusual features can sometimes be. She wore all black— tight pants that outlined a very fit body and a knit black top that twisted around her in an alluring way. And that gold charm bracelet, now glinting against the black sleeve of her top.

"Hello again," I said, sliding a menu onto the table.

"I'll have exactly what I had yesterday."

"Green tea, egg salad?"

"Right."

I brought the tea and sandwich a few minutes later, and later still refilled her hot water when I was asked. When she had finished and I went to clear her plate, she invited me to join her at the table. I froze.

"Just for a second," she said, nudging the chair across from her.

"I'm working," I said, feeling clenched and a little cornered. I could see Dell in the kitchen through the cutout window behind the bar. What if this woman asked me questions about the notebook?

"I'm sure Will won't mind if you sit a bit," Matilda said. "Besides, the place is empty."

"You know Will?" I said, sinking slowly into the chair.

"I know a lot of people, Cassie. But I don't know you."

"Well, I'm not that interesting. I'm just me. I'm just a waitress and . . . that's it, really."

"No woman's just a waitress, or just a teacher, or just a mother."

"I *am* just a waitress. I guess I'm a widow too. But mostly I am just a waitress."

"A widow? I'm sorry to hear that. You're not originally from New Orleans. I detect a slight Midwestern accent. Illinois?"

"Close. Michigan. We moved here about six years ago. My husband and I. Before he died. Obviously. Um, how do you know Will?"

"I knew his dad. He owned this place before—it's twenty years ago now that he died, I think. Probably the last time I was a regular here. It hasn't changed much," she said, looking around.

"Will says he's going to renovate. Expand upstairs. But it's expensive. And right now it's all any restaurant can do in this city to stay open."

"That's true."

She glanced down at her hands and I got a better look at her bracelet, which seemed to have a lot more charms than Pauline's. I was going to comment on its beauty, but Matilda spoke again.

"So, Cassie, I need to ask you something. That book that . . . *Dell* found. My friend is a little worried that someone might have read it. It's a diary of sorts with lots of very personal stuff in it. Do you think Dell would have read it?"

"Oh God, no!" I said, with a little too much conviction. "Dell's not the type."

"The type? What do you mean by that?"

"Well, I mean, she's not nosy. She's not really interested in other people's lives. Just this place, the Bible, maybe her grandkids."

"Do you think it would be odd to ask Dell? To see if she read the book or showed it to anyone? It's important that we know."

Oh God! Why didn't we get a story straight? How *Dell* found the booklet, and how *she* stored it in her work locker until its rightful owner was found? Because I never thought there'd be an interrogation, that's why. Just a grateful owner making a beeline out of the restaurant, never to be seen again. Now this Matilda woman had my guts in a vise grip.

"She's *super* busy right now, but why don't I go back there and ask her?"

"Oh, I don't mind asking her myself," she said, rising from the table. "I'll just go poke my head in the back—"

"Wait!"

Matilda slowly sat back down, her eyes homing in on me.

"*I* found the journal."

Matilda's face relaxed a little, but she made no reply. She just clasped her hands on the table and leaned in a little closer.

I looked around the empty Café and continued. "I'm sorry I lied. I just, I read a little bit of it—but only to find a name, some sort of contact information. But I swear, you can tell Pauline I stopped after a page . . . or two. And, well, I was . . . embarrassed, I guess. I didn't want her to be any more uncomfortable than she already seemed. So I lied. I'm sorry. I feel like such an idiot."

"Don't feel bad. On Pauline's behalf, I thank you for returning the book to her. Our only request is that you say nothing about what you read, to anyone. Absolutely nothing. Can I trust you to do that?"

"Of course. I would never. You have nothing to worry about."

"Cassie, you don't understand how important this is. You must keep this secret." Matilda pulled a twenty from her wallet. "Here's for lunch. Keep the change."

"Thank you," I said.

Then she proffered a card with her name on it. "If you have any questions about what you read in that book, I urge you to call me. I mean it. Otherwise I won't be back here. Nor will Pauline. This is how to reach me. Day or night."

"Oh. Okay," I said, holding the card cautiously as if it were radioactive. *Matilda Greene*, and her phone number. On the back was an acronym, *S.E.C.R.E.T.*, and three sentences: *No Judgments. No Limits. No Shame.* "Are you, like, a therapist or something?"

"You could say that. I work with women who reach a crossroads in life. Usually midlife, but not always."

"Like a life coach?"

"Kind of. More like a guide."

"Do you work with Pauline?"

"I don't talk about my clients."

"I could probably use some guidance." Had I said that out loud? "But I can't afford it." Yes, I had.

"Well, this might surprise you, but you *can* afford what I charge because I work for free. The catch is I get to choose my clients."

"What do those letters stand for?"

"You mean *S.E.C.R.E.T.*? That, my dear, is a secret," she said, a sly smile playing across her lips. "But if you meet with me again, I'll tell you all about it."

"Okay."

"You're someone I'd like to hear from. And I mean that."

I knew I was wearing my skeptical expression, the one that made me look a lot like my father, the man who had told me that nothing in life's free, nor is it ever fair.

Matilda stood up from the table. When she put out her hand for me to shake, her bracelet glinted in the sun.

"Cassie, it was quite lovely to meet you. And now you have my card. Thank you for your honesty."

"Thank you for . . . not thinking I'm a complete idiot."

She let go of my hand and cupped my chin like a mother would. I could hear the charms tinkle against each other, they were so close to my ears.

"I hope we meet again."

The door chime signaled her goodbye. I knew that if I didn't call her, I'd never see her again, which made me feel unaccountably sad. I placed the card carefully in my front pouch.

"Making new friends, I see," Will said from behind the bar. He was emptying a case of sparkling water into the refrigerator.

"What's wrong with that? I could use a few friends."

"That woman's a little off. She's like a Wiccan-hippy-vegan or something. My dad knew her back in the day."

"Yeah, she told me."

Will began a long diatribe about stocking more non-alcoholic beverages because people are drinking a lot less, but that we could charge more for sparkling water and those special sodas and ciders and probably still make good margins, but all I was thinking about was Pauline's journal, and the two men, the one behind her and the one beneath her, and the way her sexy boyfriend traced his firm hands down her forearm and how he pulled her into his embrace on the street in front of everyone—

"Cassie!"

"What? What is it?" I said, shaking my head. "Jesus, you scared me."

"Where did you go just now?"

"Nowhere, I'm here. I've been here all along," I said.

"Well, go home, then. You look tired."

"I'm not tired," I said, and it was true. "In fact, I don't think I've ever been more awake."

III

t took me a week to call Matilda. A week of the same old thing, of walking to work and of walking home, of not shaving my legs, of yanking my hair into a ponytail, of feeding Dixie, of watering the plants, of ordering takeout, of drying dishes, of sleeping, and then of waking and doing it all over again. It was a week of looking out over Marigny at dusk from my third-story window, realizing that loneliness had blotted out any other feeling. It had become to me like water to a fish.

If I had to describe what propelled me to call Matilda, I guess I could say it felt as if my body was having none of this anymore. Even as my mind was reeling with the idea of asking for help, my body forced me to pick up the kitchen phone at the Café and dial.

"Hello, Matilda? This is Cassie Robichaud, from Café Rose?"

Five Years pricked up its ears.

She didn't seem at all surprised to hear from me. We had a brief conversation about work and the weather, and then

I made an appointment for the next afternoon at her office in the Lower Garden District, on Third, near Coliseum.

"It's the small white coach house next to the big mansion on the corner," she said, as though I'd know exactly where that was. In fact I always avoided the tourist spots, crowds, people in general, but I said I'd have no trouble finding it. "There's a buzzer at the gate. Give yourself a couple of hours. The first consultation's always the longest."

Dell entered the kitchen as I tore the address off the back of the paper menu on which I wrote it. She peered sternly over her reading glasses at me.

"What?" I barked.

What kind of help was this Matilda woman going to offer? I had no idea, but if it was the kind that would end with an ardent man sitting across from me at a table, it was the kind of help I welcomed. Still, I worried. *Cassie, you don't know who this woman is. You're okay on your own. You don't need anyone. You're fine.* That was my mind talking, but my body told it to shut up. And that was the end of that.

The day of our meeting I left my shift early, instead of waiting for Tracina or Will. As soon as the dining room died, I yelled goodbye to Dell and headed home to shower. From the back of the closet, I pulled out the white sundress I had bought for my thirtieth birthday. Scott had stood me up that night, and I hadn't worn it since. Five years in the South had darkened my skin and four years of waitressing had toned my arms, so I was shocked to see that it actually looked better on me now. Standing in front of the full-length mirror, I kept a hand over my nervous stomach. Why was I nauseous? Because I knew I was letting something into my life, some element of excitement, maybe even danger? I tried to recall those steps from the journal, *Surrender, Generosity, Fearlessness, Courage.* I couldn't remember them all, but pondering them this last week had created such an incredible pull, straight from the gut, that making that phone call had been more a compulsion than a decision.

The Magazine Street bus was packed with tourists and cleaning ladies heading to the Garden District. I got off at Third, stopping in front of a bar called Tracey's. I contemplated putting back a couple of shots to steel my nerves. Scott and I had done the Garden District tour when we first moved here, gawking at the colorful mansions, the pink Greek Revivals, the ones with Italianate architecture, the wrought-iron gates and the obvious money oozing everywhere. New Orleans was a study in contrasts. Rich neighborhoods next to poor ones, the ugly next to the beautiful. It frustrated Scott, but I liked that about this city. It was all extremes.

I headed north. At Camp Street, I got confused. Had I gone too far in the wrong direction? I stopped abruptly, causing a small pileup.

"I'm so sorry," I said, to an alarmed young woman behind me holding the hands of a child and a dirty-faced toddler. I continued up Third, staying closer to the houses to let a group of tourists pass me.

Turn around, Cassie, and go home. You don't need help.

But I do! One meeting. One, maybe two hours with Matilda. What could it possibly hurt?

Cassie, what if they make you do awful things? Things you don't want to do?

That's ridiculous. That's not going to happen.

How do you know?

Because Matilda was kind to me. She peered into my loneliness and didn't laugh at it. She made me feel like it was a temporary condition, perhaps even curable.

If you're so lonely, why don't you just go to bars like everyone else?

Because I'm afraid.

Afraid? And this *is less scary?*

"Yes, frankly it is!" I mumbled.

"Cassie? Is that you?" I turned around. It was Matilda on the sidewalk behind me, a line of concern across her brow. She was carrying a plastic bag in one hand and a clutch of gladiolas in the other. "Are you all right? Did you have trouble finding the place?"

I was absently clutching a wrought-iron gate, using it either to hold me up or to hold me in place.

"Oh my goodness. Hi. Yes. No. I guess I'm a little early. I thought I'd sit for a bit."

"You're right on time, actually. Come, let's go in and I'll get you something cold to drink. It's a hot one."

I had no choice now. I couldn't turn back. All I had to do was follow this woman through the gate, into which she was now punching an elaborate security code. I glanced down

Third and watched Five Years slink off without looking back at me.

I followed Matilda through a lush courtyard with overgrown vines and trees. My mind was still holding on to my mother's legs like a scared toddler. We were heading for the red door of a quaint, white coach house to the left of a massive mansion that had been barely visible from the street. A wave of dizziness rolled over me.

"Stop. Wait. I don't know if I can do this, Matilda."

"Do what, Cassie?" She turned to face me, the red flowers framing her face, setting off her red hair.

"This, whatever *this* is."

She laughed. "Why don't you find out what *this* is and then make up your mind—how about that?"

I stood still, my palms soaked in sweat. I resisted wiping them on my dress.

"You can say no, Cassie. I'm only offering. Ready?" She seemed bemused more than impatient.

"Yes," I said, and I was. Enough equivocating. I shut off my reluctant mind, or rather, I opened it.

Matilda led. I followed. My eyes were drawn back to the ivy-covered mansion and its riotous garden. April in New Orleans meant vines and flowers in full bloom. Magnolia trees blossomed so quickly it was like they had thrown on ornate '50s bathing caps overnight. I had never seen a garden this lush, green and vivid.

"Who lives there?" I asked.

"That's the Mansion. Only members are allowed inside."

I counted a dozen dormers, ornate ironwork suspended over the windows like lace bangs. The turret was topped with a white crown. Though it was all white, it had an eerie feel, like it was haunted, but perhaps by very attractive ghosts.

After we reached the coach house and Matilda entered yet another security code, we passed through a big red door and were inside. I was hit by a blast of air-conditioning. If the exterior was nondescript and blocky, the coach house interior was a study in mid-century minimalism. The windows were small, but the walls high and white. On them hung several stunning floor-to-ceiling paintings of vivid reds and pinks, dotted with yellows and blues. Tea candles flickered on the windowsills, giving the place the atmosphere of an expensive spa. I relaxed my shoulders, which had been hunched up to my ears. Nothing bad could happen in a place like this, I thought. It was so pristine. At the end of the room stood a set of doors that must have been ten feet tall. A young woman with a sharp black bob and black thick-rimmed glasses stood up from her desk and greeted Matilda.

"The Committee will be here shortly," she said, rushing around the desk to grab the groceries and flowers from Matilda's hands.

"Thanks, Danica. Danica, this is Cassie."

Committee? Was I interrupting a meeting? I felt my heart fall into my stomach.

"So nice to finally meet you," Danica said. Matilda gave her a stern look.

What did she mean by *finally*?

Danica hit a button below her desk and a door opened behind her, exposing a small brightly lit room lined in walnut, with a round plush pink rug in the center.

"My office," Matilda said. "Come in."

It was a cozy space, facing a lush courtyard, with a glimpse of the street just visible beyond the gate. From her office window I could also see the side door of the imposing Mansion next door, a maid in uniform sweeping the steps. I took a seat in a wide black armchair, the kind that makes you feel like you're being cradled in King Kong's palm.

"Do you know why you're here, Cassie?" Matilda asked.

"No, I don't. Yes. No, sorry. I don't know." I wanted to cry.

Matilda took a seat behind her desk, rested her chin in her hands and waited for me to finish. The silence was painful.

"You're here because you read something in Pauline's journal that compelled you to get in touch with me, is that right?"

"I think so. Yes," I said. I looked around the room for another door, one that could lead me to the courtyard and away from this place.

"What is it that you think compelled you?"

"It wasn't just the book," I blurted out. Through the window I noticed a couple of women entering the courtyard gate.

"What was it, then?"

I thought of my couple, their arms entwined. I thought of the notebook, of Pauline backing towards the bed, and the man—

"It was Pauline, the way she is with men. With her boyfriend. I've never been like that with anyone, not even my husband. And no one has ever been like that with me. She seems so . . . free."

"And you want that?"

"I do. I think. Is that something you work on?"

"That's the *only* thing we work on," she said. "Now, why don't we start with you. Tell me a little bit about yourself."

I don't know why it all felt so easy, but my story poured from my mouth. I told Matilda about growing up in Ann Arbor. How my mother died when I was young, and how my dad, an industrial fence contractor, was rarely around, and when he was, he was by turns sour or overly affectionate, especially when he was drunk. I grew up cautious and alert to how the weather in a room could change. My sister, Lila, left home as soon as she could and moved to New York. We barely spoke now.

Then I told Matilda about Scott, sweet Scott and sorrowful Scott, the Scott who slow-danced with me to country music in our kitchen and the Scott who hit me twice and never stopped begging forgiveness I couldn't give. I told her how our marriage deteriorated as his drinking escalated. I told her how his death hadn't liberated me but rather had relegated me to a quiet middle ground, a safe corral of my own making. I had no idea how badly I needed to talk to another woman, how isolated I'd become, until I started opening up to Matilda.

Then, I said it. It just kind of spilled out: the fact that it had been years since I'd had sex.

"How many years?"

"Five. Almost six, I guess."

"It's not uncommon. Grief, anger, resentment play awful tricks on the body."

"How do you know? Are you a sex therapist?"

"Sort of," she said. "What we do here, Cassie, is we help women get back in touch with their sexual side. And in so doing, they get back in touch with the most powerful part of themselves. One Step at a time. Does that interest you?"

"I guess. Sure," I said, as squeamish as the time I had to tell my dad I had started my period. With no woman in the house growing up, except for my dad's listless girlfriend, I'd never actually spoken about sex out loud with anyone.

"Will I have to do anything . . . weird?"

Matilda laughed.

"No. Nothing weird, Cassie, unless that's your thing."

I laughed then, too, the uncomfortable laugh of someone past the point of no return.

"But what do I do? How does this work?"

"You don't really have to do anything but say yes to the Committee," she said, glancing at her watch, "which, my goodness, is assembling as we speak."

"The Committee?" Oh my God, what had I *done*? It was like I'd fallen down a deep hole.

Matilda must have sensed my panic. She poured me a glass of water from the jug on her desk.

"Here, Cassie, take a drink, and please try to relax. This is a good thing. A marvelous thing, trust me. The Committee is simply a group of women, kind women, many of them just like you, women who want to help. They recruit partici-pants and design the fantasies. The Committee makes your fantasies happen."

"*My* fantasies? What if I don't have any?"

"Oh, you do. You just don't know it yet. And don't worry. You will never have to do anything you don't want to do, nor will you ever be with anyone you don't want to be with. S.E.C.R.E.T.'s motto is: No judgments. No limits. No shame."

The water glass shook in my hand. I took a big gulp and choked.

"S.E.C.R.E.T.?"

"Yes, that's what our group is called. Each letter stands for something. But our whole reason for being is liberation through complete submission to your sexual fantasies."

I stared into the middle distance, trying to shake the image of Pauline with two men . . .

"Is this what Pauline did?" I blurted out.

"Yes. Pauline completed all ten steps of S.E.C.R.E.T., and now is living in the world, fully, sexually alive."

"Ten?"

"Well, technically there are nine fantasies. The tenth Step is a decision. You can either stay in S.E.C.R.E.T. for one year, recruiting other women like you, training fantasy participants, or helping other members facilitate fantasies. Or you can decide to bring your sexual knowledge into your own world, perhaps into a loving relationship."

Over Matilda's right shoulder through the courtyard window, I could see more women of various ages, colors and sizes filing by twos and threes through the gate. I could hear them entering the lobby, laughing and chatting.

"Is that the Committee?"

"Yes. Shall we join them?"

"Wait. This is all moving a little too fast. I need to ask: if I say yes, what exactly happens then?"

"Everything you want. Nothing you don't," she replied. "Yes or no, Cassie. It really is that simple."

My body was all in, but my mind finally freed itself from its temporary restraints and unleashed its doubts.

"But I don't even *know* you! I don't know who you are, who those women are. And I'm supposed to sit here and tell you my deepest, most private sex fantasies? And I don't even know that I have any, let alone *nine*, since I've only ever slept with *one* man, my whole life, ever. So how can I say yes or no to *any* of this?"

Matilda remained placid through my little rant, the way a good mother will stay present during a toddler's tantrum. Nothing I said could turn my body around and take it home now, and I knew it. So did she. My poor mind was losing this fight.

"Yes or no, Cassie," Matilda said again.

I looked around the room, at the bookshelf behind me, the antique windows facing the courtyard, the wall of hedges, then back to Matilda's kind face. I needed to be touched. I needed to let a man loose on my body before it died a slow and lonely death. This felt like something that had to be done *to* me. *With* me.

"Yes."

She gently clapped her hands once.

"I'm so glad. Oh, and it's supposed to be fun, Cassie. It *will* be fun!"

With that, Matilda removed a small booklet from her desk drawer and slid it in front of me. It had the same burgundy cover as Pauline's journal, only it was longer and thinner, like a checkbook.

"I am going to leave you alone so you can fill out this brief questionnaire. It will give us a sense of what you're looking for, of what you . . . like. And where you're at. You will write down specific fantasies later. But this is a start. Take fifteen minutes. Just be honest. I'll come get you when you're done. The Committee is assembling. Tea? Coffee?"

"Tea would be nice," I said, feeling very tired.

"Cassie, fear is the only thing that stands between you and your real life. Remember that."

After she left, I was so jittery that I couldn't even look at the booklet. I got up and walked over to a bookshelf at the back of the office. What I thought was a set of encyclopedias turned out to be bound copies of *The Complete Kama Sutra*, *The Joy of Sex*, *Lady Chatterley's Lover*, *My Secret Garden*, *The Happy Hooker*, *Fanny Hill*, and the *Story of O*, some of the books I used to find at the homes where I babysat when I was a teenager, books I'd scan and that would leave me confused as I was driven home by the parents late at night.

They were bound in the same burgundy leather as the booklet and journal, the titles embossed in gold. I ran a finger across them, took a deep breath, and then went back to my seat.

I sat down and opened the booklet.

What you have in your hands is completely confidential. Your answers are for you and for the Committee only. No one else will see your responses. For S.E.C.R.E.T. to help you, we must know more about you. Be thorough, be honest, be fearless. Please begin:

What followed was a list of questions, with space between each for the answers. The questions made me dizzy with their specificity. Just as I tested the pen, there was a soft knock at the door.

"Come in?"

Danica's black bob peered around the door. "Sorry to interrupt," she said. "Matilda said you wanted some tea?"

"Oh, thanks."

She entered and gently placed a silver tea set in front of me.

"Danica, have you done this? This *thing*?"

She smiled a big smile.

"Nope. See?" she said, holding up her bare wrist. "No bracelet for me. That's how you know. Matilda says I may never need to join if I play my cards right from the start with my boyfriend. Plus, you have to be, like, old—over thirty. But I think it's really cool," she added, every inch the twenty-one-or-two-year-old she probably was. "Just answer honestly, Cassie. Everything after that will be easy. That's what Matilda always says."

Then she turned and walked out, closing the door behind her and leaving me alone again with the questionnaire and my racing mind. *You can do this, Cassie.* And so I began.

1. *How many lovers have you had? Who is your ideal lover physically? Please specify height, weight, hair color, penis size and any other physical preferences.*
2. *Can you reach orgasm through vaginal sex?*
3. *Do you enjoy oral sex (getting)? Do you enjoy oral sex (giving)? Explain.*
4. *How often do you masturbate? Preferred method?*
5. *Have you ever had a one-night stand?*
6. *Do you tend to make the first move when you are attracted to someone?*
7. *Have you had sex with a woman, or with more than one partner at the same time? Explain.*
8. *Have you had anal sex? Did you enjoy it? If not, why not?*
9. *What type of birth control do you use?*
10. *What do you consider your personal erogenous zones?*
11. *What are your thoughts on pornography?*

And on and on and on. *Do you enjoy sex on your period? Dirty talk? S&M? Bondage? Lights on or off?* . . . This was what I had been most afraid of: feeling over my head. It was like those awful dreams of surprise quizzes that I was plagued by after I left university. I had had exactly *one* sex partner. I had no idea about penis preference, and anal sex was an exotic, remote idea, up there with tattooing my face and shoplifting. But I had to answer honestly. What's the worst thing that could happen? That they would discover my complete sexual ineptitude and usher me to the door? Thinking about that made the rest of the exercise seem ludicrously fun. After all, what did I have to lose? After all, wasn't I here because of my sexual inexperience?

I started with the simplest question, the first one, which was easy enough—*One*. I have had *one* lover. Scott. One. And only one. As for my physical type, I thought of all the movie stars and musicians that I found attractive and surprised myself by filling the entire space with names and ideals. Then I moved on to the next question: vaginal orgasms? I skipped it. I had no idea. The one about erogenous zones almost had me scanning the bookshelf for a dictionary. I couldn't answer that. Nor the next one, nor the one about being with women. I answered the rest as best I could. Finally I turned to the last page in the booklet, where there was a blank space for me to add any other thoughts.

I am trying hard to answer these questions, but I have only had sex with my husband. We mostly did it missionary style. Maybe two times a week when we first got married. After that, maybe once a month. The light was often off. Sometimes I had an orgasm . . . I think. I'm not sure; maybe I was faking. Scott never went down on me. I have . . . touched myself now and again. It's been a long time since I've done that, though. Scott always wanted me to put him in my mouth. I did it, for a while, but I couldn't do that again after he hit me. I couldn't do anything with him after he hit me. He died almost four years ago. It has been longer than that since I last had sex. I am sorry, but I can't finish this test, even though I'm trying my best.

I put down my pen and closed the booklet. Even writing what I had made me feel a little unburdened.

I didn't hear Matilda slip back into the room.

"How did you do?" she asked as she returned to her desk and sat down.

"Not very well, I'm afraid."

She picked up the booklet. I had the strongest urge to rip it from her hands and hold it to my chest.

"You know, it's not the kind of test you can fail," she said, a sad smile crossing her face as she quickly scanned my answers. "All right, then. Cassie, come with me. Time to meet the Committee."

I felt welded to my big comfortable chair. I knew that if I crossed the threshold of this room, another chapter of my life would unfold. Was I ready?

Strangely, I was. With each gesture, it felt more doable. Maybe that's what the ten steps would feel like. I kept reminding myself that nothing bad was happening to me. Quite the opposite. I felt like layers of ice were falling away.

We left the room together and crossed the reception area, where Danica hit another button beneath her desk. The giant white doors at the end parted to reveal a large oval table made of glass, around which about a dozen women sat chatting loudly. The room was windowless, and also white, with a few colorful paintings similar to the ones in the lobby. There was a portrait at the far end, above a wide mahogany console, of a beautiful dark-skinned woman with a long braid falling forward over her shoulder. We entered the room and the women fell silent.

"Everybody, this is Cassie Robichaud."

"Hi, Cassie," they sang.

"Cassie, this is the Committee."

I opened my mouth to speak, but nothing came out.

"Sit here next to me, my dear," said a small Indian woman, easily in her sixties, wearing a vivid sari and a very kind smile. She pulled out a chair and patted it.

"Thank you," I said, and sank into the seat. I wanted to look everyone in the face, and at the same time to look at no one. I alternated between clasping my hands tightly in my lap and firmly sitting on them, trying hard to keep myself from fidgeting like a teenage girl. *You are thirty-five, Cassie, grow up.*

As Matilda introduced each woman, her voice sounded far away and underwater. My eyes floated from face to face, lingering, as I tried to memorize their names. I noted how each was a different kind of beautiful.

There was Bernice, a red-headed black woman, round, short and busty. She was young. Maybe thirty. There were a couple of blondes, one tall named Daphne, with straight long hair, and the other named Jules, with short perky curls. There was a curvy brunette woman named Michelle, with an angelic face, who clasped her hands over her mouth like I had done something adorable at a dance recital. She leaned over and whispered to a woman sitting across from me named Brenda, who had a toned, athletic body and was dressed in gym clothes. Roslyn with the long auburn hair was next to her. She had the biggest brown eyes I'd ever seen. There were also two Hispanic women sitting side by side, identical twins. Maria had a look in her eyes that was determined; Marta seemed more serene and open. It was then that I noticed each of the women at the table wore a familiar gold charm bracelet.

"And finally, next to you is Amani Lakshmi, who has been on the Committee the longest. In fact, she was my guide, as I will be yours," said Matilda.

"So very nice to meet you, Cassie," she said with a slight accent, lifting her slender arm to shake my hand. I saw that she was the only one in the room wearing two bracelets, one on each wrist. "Before we start, do you have any questions?"

"Who's the woman in the painting?" I heard myself say.

"Carolina Mendoza, the woman who made all of this possible," Matilda said.

"Who still does," added Amani.

"Yes, that's true. As long as we have her paintings, we have the means to continue S.E.C.R.E.T. in New Orleans."

Matilda explained how she met Carolina more than thirty-five years earlier, back when she was an arts administrator for the city. Carolina was an artist, originally from Argentina. She fled in the '70s, just before the military crackdown made it impossible for artists and feminists to create and speak freely. They met at an art auction. She was just beginning to show her work, large vivid canvases and murals that weren't typical of the paintings women were doing at the time.

"Are these her paintings? And the ones in the lobby?" I asked.

"Yes. Which is why security is so tight here. Each is worth millions. We have a few more in storage in the Mansion."

Matilda explained how she and Carolina began to spend time together, something that surprised Matilda because she hadn't made a new friend in a long time.

"It wasn't a sexual relationship, but we talked an awful lot about sex. After a while she trusted me enough to share her world with me, a secret world where women gathered to talk about their deepest desires, their most hidden fantasies. Remember, it wasn't common back then to talk about sex. Let alone how much you liked it."

At first Carolina's group was informal, Matilda said, a gathering of artist friends, and local offbeat characters, which have always been aplenty in New Orleans. Most were single, some were widows, a few were long married, some of them happily so, she said. Most were successful and over thirty. But there was something missing from their marriages, their lives.

Matilda became her exclusive art broker and Carolina's paintings began selling for sky-high prices. Eventually she sold several to the American wife of a Middle-Eastern oil sheik for tens of millions of dollars. She bought the Mansion next door, then put the rest of her fortune into a trust that funded their burgeoning sexual collective.

"Ultimately we realized we wanted to *experience* our sexual fantasies—all of them. And these scenarios cost money. Finding men, and sometimes women, the *right* men and women, to fulfill these fantasies, required recruiting. And . . . training. That's how S.E.C.R.E.T. began.

"After we all helped one another experience *our* sexual fantasies, we began recruiting one person every year upon whom we would bestow this gift—the gift of complete sexual emancipation. As current chair of the Committee, it was my duty to choose this year's recruit. According to our mandate, she must, in turn, choose us."

"That's your cue, Cassie," said Brenda.

"Me? Why?"

"For several reasons. We have been watching you for a while now. Pauline made the suggestion after seeing you at the restaurant. She didn't leave her notebook on purpose, but we couldn't have planned it better. We had already discussed you a couple of times. It all worked out rather well."

This stunned me for a moment, that I'd been watched, checked out . . . for what? Signs of abject loneliness? I felt a flash of anger.

"What are you saying exactly? That you saw I was some pathetic, lonely waitress?" I looked accusingly around the room.

Amani reached out and held my arm, while some of the women murmured reassurances: "No" and "It's not like that" and "Oh, honey, that's not what we meant."

"Cassie, it's not an insult. We operate from a spirit of love and support. When someone shuts down their sexual self prematurely, it's often not noticeable to them. But other people pick up on it. It's like you're operating with one less sense. Only you don't know it. Sometimes people in that kind of retreat need an intervention of sorts. That's all. That's what I meant. We found you. We picked you for this. And now we're offering you a chance at a new beginning. An awakening. If you want it. Do you want to join us and begin your journey?"

I was stuck on how they had been *monitoring* me. *How?* I had always thought I camouflaged my loneliness, my accidental celibacy. Then I remembered my brown clothing, my messy ponytail, my awful shoes, my slouch, my cat, my trudge home at dusk to my empty apartment. Anyone with a set of eyes could have seen that a brown-colored aura had settled over me, like a dusting of defeat. It was time. Time to make a leap.

"Yes," I said, shaking the remaining doubt out of my head. "I'm in. I want to do this."

The room erupted in applause. Amani nodded encouragingly.

"Consider the women in this circle your sisters. We can guide you back to your true self," Matilda said, standing up.

My chest tightened with emotion. I was feeling so much at the same time—joy, fear, confusion and gratitude. Was this really happening? To me?

"Why are you doing this for me?" I asked, tears pooling in the corners of my eyes.

"Because we can," said Bernice.

Matilda reached under the table and pulled a zippered folder. She placed it in front of me. It looked like real alligator skin and it was embossed with my initials, *CR*. They knew, on some fundamental level, that this was not something I could turn down. I opened it, exposing the two sides of the folder, each filled with ornately embossed papers. On the left was a linen envelope with my name on it in calligraphy. Even my wedding invitations weren't this beautiful.

"Go ahead," said Matilda. "Open it."

I carefully ripped the seal. Inside was a card.

On this day, Cassie Robichaud is invited by the Committee to take the Steps.

_____ *Cassie Robichaud*

Beneath that was another line:

_____ *Matilda Greene, Guide*

Tucked into the right side of the folder was a small journal, exactly like Pauline's, also with my initials.

"Cassie, would you read the Steps aloud for us?"

"Now?" I looked around the table and couldn't see a single face that frightened me, and I knew that I could walk out the door at any time—but I didn't want to. I stood up, but my legs felt frozen. "I'm scared."

"Every one of the women around this table has felt the same thing you're feeling right now," Matilda said, and the women nodded. "Cassie, we *are* our sexual lives."

The tears were flowing now. It felt, at long last, as though all the grief I'd stored up in me was finally finding its way out.

Amani leaned closer to me and said, "The ability to heal ourselves has made it possible for us to help others. That's why we're here. That's the *only* reason we're here."

I stared down at the diary. I gathered every ounce of strength and courage I could muster. I wanted to come alive like these women. I wanted to feel pleasure, and to live in my body again. I wanted all of it. I wanted everything. I opened to the Steps and read all ten, the same words I had read in Pauline's diary. When I finished, I sat down and a great sense of relief moved from my feet, through my body, and out my arms.

"Thank you, Cassie," Matilda said. "Now I have three important questions for you. One, do you want what we have?"

"Yes," I said.

"Two, within the boundaries of complete safety and security and the guidance we offer you, are you willing to take these Steps?"

I looked back down at the Steps. I wanted this. I really did. "Yes. I think so."

"And three, Cassie Robichaud, do you accept me as your guide?"

"Yes. I do," I said.

The room burst into more applause.

Matilda squeezed my hands in hers. "Cassie, I promise you that you'll be safe, you'll be cared for, you'll be cherished. You have total autonomy over your body and what you want to do with it. You can decide how to proceed at all times. You will never be coerced. That's not to say you won't be afraid, but that's what we're here for. What I'm here for. Now I have one more thing to give you."

She walked over to the console, above which hung the portrait of Carolina. She opened the slender top drawer and carefully removed a small purple box. She carried it to me like it was the most fragile thing on earth. But when she placed it in my hands, the box felt surprisingly heavy.

"Open it. It's for you."

I lifted the velvet top, and under a downy bit of fluff lay a pale gold chain nestled in silk. It was identical to the one everyone else in the room was wearing. But this was only a bare chain—no charms were attached.

"It's mine?"

Matilda lifted it out of the box and fastened it around my trembling wrist.

"For every Step you complete, Cassie, you will receive a gold charm from me commemorating its completion.

S . E . C . R . E . T .

This will continue until you have received all nine charms. The tenth charm comes after you make your choice to stay in S.E.C.R.E.T. or to leave. Are you ready to begin your adventure?"

The bracelet made it all feel real, its very weight grounding me, making me conscious of the magnitude of what had just occurred, and what was about to.

"I'm ready."

IV

was vibrating from head to toe on my way home, thinking about the task ahead of me. Matilda had sent me away with the folder and told me it included nine pages, one page per fantasy. I was supposed to fill these out right away and call Danica as soon as I was done, presumably so she could send a courier to fetch the papers. The last thing Matilda said to me was, "As soon as we get those papers, it will all begin. You and I will speak after every fantasy. But don't hesitate to call me, for anything, in between, okay?"

In my apartment I scooped up Dixie and gave her kisses all over her belly. Then I lit a lot of candles, undressed and soaked in a sweet-smelling bath. All of this was supposed to help me conjure the best possible fantasy list. I found my favorite pen and whipped out the first page from my alligator folder. I felt a stirring in me that I hadn't felt in years. Matilda had instructed me to lay it bare, to lay out all my sexual longings. Everything I'd ever wanted to do or try. She told me not to judge, not to question.

"Don't get too descriptive, don't think too much. Just write." There weren't rules for the fantasies, she explained, but the letters in *S.E.C.R.E.T.* represented their criteria, which they took great pains to adhere to. Matilda said each fantasy must feel:

S afe, in that the participant feels no danger.

E rotic, in that the fantasy is sexual in nature, not just imaginary.

C ompelling, in that the participant truly wants to complete the fantasy.

R omantic, in that the participant feels wanted and desired.

E cstatic, in that the participant experiences joy in the act.

T ransformative, in that something in the participant changes in a fundamental way.

I looked at the acronym again and absently wrote a word beneath each of the first few letters, something so apt that it made me laugh out loud: **S**exual **E**mancipation of **C**assie **R**obichaud. For the final **E** and **T** all I could think to write was **E**xciting **T**imes. This really was happening. To me!

With Dixie circling my ankles and candles flickering on the table, I began by ticking off the box next to the sentence: *I want to be serviced.* I wasn't sure what it meant, but I ticked it anyhow. Could it be something about oral sex? I suggested it once to Scott and he crinkled his nose in a way that shut down the request forever. I had put away that longing in a high drawer, never to be seen again. Or so I thought. There were many other kinds of sex I'd never had too. I had a college friend who raved about doing it "the other way," and it always left me curious. I could never have asked Scott to try something like that. And I wasn't even sure if it was something I wanted.

I want to have secret sex, in public. Another check.

I want to be taken by surprise. This thrilled me a little, even though, again, I wasn't sure what it meant. I had been assured I'd be safe, that I could stop anything whenever I wanted. I ticked the box.

I want to be with someone famous. What? How could they pull that off? This seemed impossible, interesting. Tick.

I want to be rescued. Rescued from what? I put a checkmark in the box.

I want to be picked to be the princess. Oh God, what woman didn't want that? I was always considered the nice one, the smart one, maybe even the funny one. But I had never been the pretty one, the princess, never in my whole life. So yes to this. Sure. Even though it sounded childish. I wanted to feel that. Just once.

I want to be blindfolded. I imagined being in the dark might be liberating, so I checked the box.

I want to have sex in an exotic place with an exotic stranger. Technically weren't they all strangers, these men I'd be with, who I'd never see again? With no talking, no speaking, just bodies brushing past each other, and then . . . maybe he'd grasp my wrist . . . Keep writing.

I want to role-play. Could I do that? Be someone else, not me? Would I have the guts? I could always back out if I had to.

So this became my list: nine fantasies that would be followed by a final decision. And, as instructed, I wrote them in the order in which I thought I could handle them.

I looked at them one last time. My head filled with all the wonder and worry and joy and fear that these fantasies would release. Imagine getting everything you ever wanted and more. Imagine being what other people want and desire—every inch of you—exactly as you are. This was happening. This was happening *to me.* I had thought my life was winding down, but it was about to change forever.

When I was done, I called Danica.

"Hello, Cassie," she said.

"How did you know it was me?" I asked, glancing uneasily out my front window.

"Er, call display?"

"Right. So I know it's late, but Matilda told me to call as soon as I was done. So I'm done—I have them . . . selected."

"What?"

"You know . . . the list."

There was silence.

"List?" she prodded.

"My . . . *fantasies,*" I whispered.

"Oh, Cassie. We definitely found the right candidate in you. You can't even say the word!" She giggled. "I'll send someone right over, sweetie. And hold tight. Things are about to get *very* interesting."

Fifteen minutes later, my front doorbell rang. I whipped it open expecting to see a scraggly teenage courier, but a lanky, good-looking man leaned against the doorjamb. He had puppy-dog brown eyes, and wore a hoodie, white T-shirt and jeans. He looked about thirty years old.

He smiled. "I'm here to fetch your folder. And I'm also instructed to give you this. You must open it now."

I couldn't make out his accent. Was it Spanish? He passed me a small cream-colored envelope. It had the letter *C* on the outside.

I slid my finger under the flap and ripped it open. Inside was a card that read: *Step One.* My heart sped up. "What does the card say?" he asked.

I looked up at this impossibly handsome man, this courier, or whatever he was, in front of me. "You want me to read it?"

"Yes, you must."

"It says . . . '*Surrender.*'" My voice was barely audible.

"You will be asked at the beginning of every fantasy if you accept this Step. Do you accept this Step?"

I gulped.

"Which Step?"

"Step One, of course. *Surrender.* You must surrender to the fact that you need help. *Sexually.*"

My God, he practically purred the word. He placed a hand under his T-shirt and touched his stomach while he leaned on the doorjamb and took me in with his eyes.

"Do you?" he asked.

I didn't know it would all begin *this* quickly.

"I . . . with you? Now?"

"Do you accept the Step?" he asked, moving ever so slightly towards me.

I could hardly speak. "What . . . what will happen?"

"Nothing, unless you accept the Step."

His eyes, the way he was leaning . . .

"I . . . yes. I do."

"Why don't you clear a space for me right there," he said, making a big circle with his hand and indicating the area between my living room and dining room. "I'll be right back." Then he turned around and left.

I ran to my living room window and saw him heading to a limo that was parked outside.

I placed my hand on my chest and glanced around my spotless living room, candles flickering everywhere. I was showered and scented. I was wearing a silk nightgown. They *knew!* I kicked the ottoman to the wall and shoved the couch closer to the coffee table.

The young man returned a minute or two later with what looked like a portable massage table.

"Please go into the bedroom and take everything off, Cassie. Put this towel around you. I will call you when I'm ready."

I gathered Dixie on the way in. This was something my cat didn't need to see. In my room I let my robe drop to the floor and took a last glance in my dresser mirror. My internal critic kicked in immediately. But this time I did something I had never done before. I shut it off. I waited, clenching and un-clenching my fists. *This can't be real. This can't be happening. But it is!*

"Please come in," I heard from behind the closed door.

I entered as timid as a mouse to a transformed room. The blinds had been shut. The candles were placed on my end tables on either side of a massage table. It was equipped with stirrups and the bottom half had a split down the middle. I reflexively pulled the towel tight around me as I tiptoed over to the table towards this impossibly handsome young man standing in the middle of my living room. He was just shy of six feet tall. His hair was shiny and wavy, long enough to tuck some of it behind his ears. His forearms were sinewy and tanned, and his hands looked muscular. Maybe he really was a massage therapist! When he rested one of his hands under his T-shirt, I caught a glimpse of his flat stomach, also tanned. He wore a knowing smile that made him look a little older, and a lot sexier. Brown eyes. Did I mention his eyes? They were almond-shaped, with a bit of mischief in them. How could a guy be both kind-looking and hot? I'd never experienced that combination before, but it was potent.

"Drop the towel. Let me look at you," he gently commanded.

I hesitated. How could I show myself to a man this attractive?

"I want to see you."

Good God, Cassie, what have you gotten yourself into? What choice did I have? There really was no turning back now. I barely met his eyes as I let the towel drop around my feet.

"My hands have a beautiful woman to work with," he said. "Please lie down. I'm here to give you a massage."

I eased onto the table and lay back. The ceiling loomed above me. I covered my face with my hands.

"I can't believe this is happening."

"It is. This is all for you."

He placed his large warm hands on my naked body and lightly pressed down on my shoulders, then urged my hands away from my face and down to my sides.

"It's okay," he said, his brown eyes smiling at me. "Nothing bad is going to happen. Quite the opposite, Cassie."

The contact felt amazing. His hands on my thirsty skin. How long had it been since I'd been touched, let alone like this? I couldn't even remember.

"Turn over onto your stomach, please."

I hesitated again. Then I rolled over, shoving my shaking arms beneath me to calm them down, turning my head to one side. He gently placed a sheet over my body.

"Thank you."

He bent over to bring his mouth close to my ear. "Don't thank me yet, Cassie."

Through the sheet, I felt his hands on my back, pressing me flat to the table.

"It's going to be okay. Close your eyes."

"I . . . it's just nerves, I guess. I didn't think it was going to happen so fast, like right now. I mean—"

"Just lie still. I'm here to make you feel good."

I felt his hands traveling down my thighs under the sheet,

then covering the backs of my knees. Then, standing at the base of the table, he split the bottom half of the table in two, like a Y, and stood between my legs.

Oh my God! I thought. *This is happening.*

"I don't know if I can do this right now," I said, trying to turn around.

"If I touch you in any way you don't like, you tell me. And I will stop. That's how this works. That's how it will always work. But, Cassie, it's just a massage."

I could hear him take something out from under the table and then I smelled the delicious perfume of coconut lotion. I heard him rubbing it on his hands. Then he clasped the backs of my ankles.

"Does this feel okay? Tell me honestly." Okay? It felt way more than okay.

"Yes," I said.

"This?" he asked, slowly moving his warm, oiled hands up the backs of my calves.

Sweet Jesus, his hands were amazing. "Yes."

"How about this? Do you like this? Tell me," he said, reaching my thighs and stopping just below my buttocks. Then he began to knead my inner thighs. I felt my legs opening up to him.

"Cassie. Do you want this?"

"Yes." *Oh God I said it.*

"Good," he said, moving his hands to the crests of my cheeks. There he began to massage in widening circles, touching me almost between my legs. Almost, but not quite. My body was in panic mode and yet highly aroused. I had never existed in this place between fear and nirvana before and it was strange, intoxicating, and wonderful.

"Do you like it firm or soft?"

"Um— "

"I mean massage, Cassie."

"Oh. Firm, I guess. No, soft," I said, my words still muffled by the table. "I don't know what I like. Is that normal?"

He laughed. "How about we try both, then?"

He squirted more lotion on his hands and rubbed them together. This time he moved up my back in a large circle, pulling the sheet off me entirely. I watched it drop to the ground beside me. I was naked.

"Take your arms out from under you and rest them over the top of the table, Cassie," he said.

I did so and began to relax into the most intense back massage I had ever had. His thumbs traced the outline of my spine from my tailbone up to my neck, then down around my rib cage, brushing by the sides of my breasts. He circled like that for several minutes, and then dipped down to circle my butt cheeks up and out. I could feel his hard-on through his jeans against the inside of my thigh. I couldn't believe it. He was feeling something for me too? I instinctively pressed back into him.

I let my legs, on the split table, fall apart even wider. It was the sweetest, oddest thing to be open to a man like that.

"Turn around, Cassie, I want you on your back."

"Okay," I said. The room was warm from the candles, or perhaps from my overheated body. Just his hands, that rub-down, had removed so much tension and anxiety. I felt completely boneless.

I did as he asked. He seemed to know exactly what he was doing. I guess this is what Matilda meant by surrender-ing. Before I left the coach house that day, she left me with one simple instruction for my first Step.

"Above all else, sex requires surrender, the ability to simply melt with each arriving moment," she said.

As I adjusted myself, I was so oiled I nearly slid off the table. Positioned where he was, between my legs, he grabbed me by the thighs to hold me firm. He took my entire body in with hungry eyes. Was he faking this? He seemed, dare I say, into me, which made the whole thing that much more enjoyable.

"You have the sweetest-looking pussy I have ever seen," he said.

"Oh, well, thank you, I guess," I replied, embarrassed, lifting one hand to cover my eyes. I was curious about what would happen next, and at the same time still incredibly shy.

"Do you want me to kiss it?"

What! This was insane. This was also marvelous, this feeling, this weird and perfect thing that was charging like a current through my body. He wasn't even touching me *there* and yet I was losing a part of my consciousness. Two weeks ago I had no idea a world like this existed, a world where sexy men knock on your door on a Wednesday night and bring you to the brink of ecstasy without even touching you. But it was real and this was happening—to me. This achingly beautiful man wanted to do this. To me!

I could have laughed and cried.

"Tell me what you want, Cassie. I have the power to give it to you. And I *want* to give it to you. Do you want me to kiss it?"

"I want you to," I said. And then I felt his hot breath on me, as his lips brushed my stomach. Oh my God, he trailed a finger down my stomach and then slid it inside me.

"You're wet, Cassie," he whispered.

I reflexively placed one hand on his head and gently grabbed a fistful of his hair.

"You do want me to kiss your sweet pussy."

That word again. Why was I so shy of it?

"Yes . . . I . . . want you to—"

"You can say it, Cassie. There's nothing wrong with saying it."

He flicked and probed with a single finger around the inside and outside of me.

Next, he placed his mouth on my stomach, and explored my belly button with his tongue. He trailed along the same path as his finger, and found me there and licked and nibbled, the whole time keeping his fingers circling around and just outside of me. I couldn't believe the sensation, like I was slowly going uphill in a roller-coaster, higher and higher. I heard him moan, just slightly. Oh God, it was like a thousand nerve endings were finally awakening.

"Cassie, I love how you taste."

Really? Was that possible?

His hands began to move up the length of my legs, spreading them farther open on the table. I had never felt so helpless, so vulnerable, before. I was exposed, all need and want. I was powerless, and happy to be so. I was on the rim of a thousand explosions, a million different sensations, and if he just kept going I would— And then he stopped.

"Why did you stop?" I cried out.

"You don't want me to stop?"

"No!"

"Then tell me what you want."

"I want to . . . come. Like this. Just like this."

His tawny skin, that face . . . I lay back down and covered my face with my hands again. I couldn't watch. Then I couldn't *not* watch. Suddenly I could feel something hot and wet circling my left nipple. His hand cupped the other breast firmly. His mouth was warm. He sucked and pulled on me, while his free hand left my breast and traveled back down over my quivering stomach, past my pubic bone and beyond. This time he slid two fingers inside me, gently at first, then urgently. Oh God, this felt so good! I tried lifting my knees to arch my back.

"Lie still," he whispered. "You like that?"

"I do, I like it so much," I said, throwing my arm up over my head, grabbing the top of the table. He stopped moving his fingers. Then he stood over me for a second, and took me in.

"You are beautiful," he said.

Then he leaned over and placed his tongue on me again. He kept still for a hot, quivering second, while his breath blew life into me. Involuntarily, I pushed into his face. He could sense my need and started to lap at me, slowly at first. Then he used his fingers again. With the weight of his mouth and tongue on me, he licked me again, releasing his juices and mine. I could feel all the blood in my body shoot straight down there. Oh sweetness, this was so crazy! An incredible surge ran through me, a storm of something I couldn't stop. He released his hands up to my breasts, while his tongue circled me at a perfect rhythm.

"Don't stop!" I heard myself say.

It was all too much. I squeezed my eyes shut. The beautiful feeling just built and built, and I was coming hard against his face and tongue. When I was done, he pulled away and placed his warm hand over my stomach.

"Breathe," he whispered.

My legs relaxed over the edge of the table. No man had ever touched me like that, ever.

"Are you okay?"

I nodded. I had no words. I tried to catch my breath.

"You must be a little thirsty."

I nodded again as a bottle of water appeared. I sat up to drink. He looked me over, seeming quite proud of himself.

"Shower off, beautiful," he said.

I peeled myself off the table.

"Who has the power?" he asked.

"I do," I said, smiling over my shoulder.

I stumbled towards the bathroom and took a hot shower, and afterwards, while towel-drying my hair, I had a realization. I ran out to the living room.

"Hey, I don't even know your name!" I said, still rubbing my wet hair dry on a towel.

But he was gone. So was the massage table and my fantasy list that he was sent to fetch. The place was exactly as it had been before he arrived, except for one difference: resting on my side table was my first gold charm. I crossed the room to get it, and caught a glimpse of my face in the mantel mirror. It looked flushed, my damp hair snaking around my neck and shoulders. I picked up the charm and dangled it in the candlelight. It was embossed with the word *Surrender* on one side, a Roman numeral I on the other.

I secured it to the chain around my wrist, feeling a boldness rise in me, making me giddy. *I did the strangest thing! The strangest thing was done to me!* I wanted to scream, *Something happened to me. Something is happening to me. And I will never be the same again.*

V

They always say that the first step is the hardest. That first surrender, the first time you say: *Yes, I accept that I need help. I can't do this alone.* Scott struggled with that when he gave up drinking. He hated the idea that he had to accept help from anything or anyone. So he fought it, whatever it was. Yet, here I was in full surrender. I had stopped fighting. I had accepted help from a strange group of women.

Then I walked into a room bathed in candlelight, wearing only a towel. I let that towel drop around my ankles, and I bared myself. I trusted this process, this man, this S.E.C.R.E.T. group. But everything that had happened occurred in my home, in my living room, and though it was my body, I gave it over only temporarily to a complete stranger. As I recounted this a week later to a rapt Matilda, I couldn't help but feel I was talking about my experience as if it had happened to another person, someone I knew very well but who had aspects I was only just beginning to understand.

I told Matilda I had felt safe, that what we did was erotic, and I was beyond compelled to complete the fantasy. And for a one-time thing, I had to admit I had felt wanted, desired, which of course makes any woman feel ecstatic.

"So, yes. I was . . . transformed, I guess," I said, burying my burning red face in my hands, suppressing a giggle. A few weeks ago, I had had no one to talk to, unless you counted Will. Now, here I was sharing intimate secrets with a woman I could no longer call a stranger. In fact, I had to admit she was becoming my friend.

During the weeks that followed my first fantasy, I was as busy as I had ever been. I even took on a couple of night shifts so Tracina and Will could go on dates. When I waved goodbye to them one of those nights, I couldn't detect an ounce of jealousy or bitterness in my bones. Well, maybe a droplet of jealousy, but no bitterness. No longing. No detectable sadness. I had made a vow to be nicer to Tracina, to try to see what Will saw in her. Maybe we'd become friends, too, I thought, and Will could make another attempt to set me up with someone—after I'd completed my Steps, of course. At that moment, while I was thinking about double dating, Dell caught me whistling in the walk-in fridge. I sometimes stood in there for a few minutes to cool down, all the while pretending to look for something.

"What are you so happy about, girl?" she asked, lisping through her missing tooth.

"Life, Dell. It's a good thing, isn't it?"

"Not always, no."

"I think it's pretty grand," I said.

"Well, goody for you," she said as I headed back to the dining area. I left her scooping out ice cream for a small birthday gathering of bankers.

My couple, my favorite fawning duo, hadn't returned since the night Pauline dropped her journal. But thoughts of their caresses were now replaced by lightning flashbacks, my own memories of that man's beautiful face between my thighs, of the hungry way he looked at me, so deliberate, so keen. I thought of his fingers, how they engaged at just the right moment, and how his firm hands guided and moved me, like I weighed nothing, like I was made of feathers—

"Cassie, for crying out loud," Dell yelled, snapping her fingers in front of my eyes. "You keep on leaving the planet."

I almost jumped out of my boring brown shoes. "Sorry!"

"Table eleven wants their bill, nine wants more coffee."

"Yes. Right," I said, noticing the two girls from table eight blankly staring at me.

Once I'd served the two tables, I went back to my thoughts. Dell had it wrong. I hadn't been fantasizing. I was remembering. Those things had actually happened. I was recalling things that had been done to me, to my body. I gave my head a healthy shake. If this is what it felt like after

Step One, what would it be like with a few more fantasies under my belt?

One day in early April, on my only day off that week, a cream-colored envelope arrived in my mailbox. There was no stamp on it. It appeared to have been hand-delivered. My heart leapt to my throat. I glanced down the street. Nobody. I ripped open the envelope. Inside was the Step Two card, and the word *Courage*. There was also a single ticket for a jazz show at Halo, a bar on the roof of The Saint Hotel, a newly built boutique hotel that was making its debut during this year's festival. Though I was no big music buff, even I knew these were hard tickets to get. I looked at the date. Tonight! This wasn't enough notice! I had nothing to wear! I did this all the time, excuses, one after the other, building and building, until the fear got so big it toppled any plan for adventure. That's how it had always worked for me. Somehow opening the door to my apartment to a stranger seemed easier to contemplate than venturing out into the hot night on my own, walking into a bar by myself, and sitting there alone, waiting for . . . what? What would I do while I waited? Read? Maybe three or four weeks is too much time between fantasies. Maybe my courage had retreated. Yet Step Two was about *Courage*, so I decided to concentrate on that, on staying open, the opposite of my usual way, which was to begin my day with the word *no* on my lips. That's how, hours later, I was trying on little black dresses, and an hour after that, sitting very still while coats of red lacquer were layered on my fingers and toenails. The whole time, I told myself I could always back out if I wanted to. I didn't have to go through with anything. I could change my mind at any time.

That evening I grabbed my fantasy folder from my night-stand. What is it about going out alone, seeing a movie alone, or enjoying dinner alone, that is so difficult? I could never bring myself to do it, preferring to rent a movie at home rather than sit alone in a darkened theater. But the alone part wasn't what I was afraid of. The alone part was easy; I'd felt alone my whole life, even when I was married. No, I was afraid that everyone else, all those people, coupled and cozy, would see me as one of The Great Unpicked, The Sadly Unselected, The Sexually Forgotten. I imagined that they would point and whisper. I imagined that they would pity me. Even I treated lone customers at the Café with extra care, like they were a little hard of hearing or something. I may even have been guilty of hovering around their tables too much, in my attempts to keep them company.

But maybe sometimes people who went out by themselves *wanted* to be alone. There are people like that: confident, soli-tary, secure with their own company. Tracina, for instance, pays someone to take her fourteen-year-old brother for ice cream every Saturday afternoon so she can lie on the couch and watch TV uninterrupted. She once told me that going to the movies alone was one of her singular pleasures.

"I get to watch what I want, eat without sharing, and I don't have to sit through the credits like Will makes me when I'm with him," she said.

But it's easy to be alone when it's a choice, harder when it's your default position.

I was feeling pure terror about entering that jazz club, when Matilda's Step Two advice rang through my head. During a pep talk over the phone, she told me, "Fear is just fear. We must take action in the face of it, Cassie, because action increases courage."

Damn it. I could do this.

I called Danica to send the limo.

"It's on the way, Cassie. Good luck," she said.

Ten minutes later the limo turned the corner at Chartres off Mandeville, stopping in front of the Spinster Hotel. Ah! I wasn't ready! Shoes in hand, I took the stairs in twos, running out barefoot past a very puzzled Anna Delmonte.

"It's the second time I've seen that limousine parked in front of the house," she said as I whizzed by. "Do you know anything about it, Cassie? It's so odd . . ."

"I'll talk to him, Anna. Don't worry. Or maybe the driver is a woman, right? You never know."

"I suppose . . ."

Without listening to the rest of her reply, I hopped into the limo and then put on my shoes. I had a funny thought: imagine if Anna knew what I was up to! I wanted to yell out: *I'm not a spinster! I'm alive for the first time in years!*

As the limo sped me to Canal, I looked down at my dress,

a snug black number, tight at the bodice, flaring out at the skirt, leaving off just below the knee. The top held me up in the right places and did a few favors for my breasts, which even to me looked full and appealing against the black contour of the halter. My shoes pinched a bit, but I knew they'd ease up as the night went on. Black pumps will go with just about everything, I told myself, rationalizing how much I'd spent on them. I had parted my hair to one side and dried it straight, holding the front in place with a gold barrette. That was the only piece of jewelry I had on, except, of course, my S.E.C.R.E.T. bracelet with its singular charm.

"You look lovely tonight, Miss Robichaud," the driver said. I had the impression S.E.C.R.E.T. staff members were told to keep a professional distance, something I imagined Danica found hard to do. She seemed so irrepressible. My "thank you" barely made it through the window opening before it closed between us.

My heart beat faster as we made turn after turn. I tried to clear my mind as Matilda had instructed. *Try not to anticipate. Try to be in the moment.*

The limo came to a stop in front of The Saint. My hand was so sweaty it slipped on the door handle, but the driver was already on the job, getting out and coming around to open the door and help me out of the back seat.

"Good luck, my dear," he said.

I nodded my appreciation and then stood for a moment, watching the beautiful people of the city stream in and out of the main doors—leggy, bold women, trailing perfume and confidence, the men, looking so proud to be seen with them. Then there was me. I realized I'd forgotten to wear perfume. My hair, pulled straight an hour ago, was starting to frizz up. The thought that this fantasy would play out in public made my fearful heart drop. That's where hearts should sit, I thought, deep in the gut, where there is more insulation to hide their anxious beating. And yet, nervous as I was, I was also . . . curious. I took a deep breath and headed inside and straight for the elevators.

A small man in a hotel uniform appeared on my left.

"Can I see your ticket?"

"Oh, yes," I said, digging in my clutch. "Here."

He eyed the ticket, then me, clearing his throat.

"Well, then," he said, pressing the up button. "Welcome to The Saint. We hope you'll enjoy your stay."

"Oh, I'm not staying here. I'm only meeting . . . well, seeing . . . *hearing*, just hearing the music."

"Of course. Have a lovely evening," he said, bowing and then backing away from me.

The elevator swallowed me up, its ascent wreaking havoc with my already churning stomach. I closed my eyes and leaned up against the cool mirrored wall, holding tight to the rail. As the elevator car neared the penthouse club, I could hear muffled music, many voices. The doors opened to dozens of smartly dressed people clustered in the dim lobby, more still in the dark bar beyond the glass doors. It took superhuman strength for me to peel my fingers from the rail, leave the safe confines of the elevator and launch myself into the crowd.

Each person was holding a glass of champagne and was engaged in what seemed to be an interesting conversation. Some women glanced over their shoulders at me the way you'd look at a potential opponent. Their male companions assessed me too. Were those looks of . . . interest? No. Couldn't be. No way. I moved slowly through the crowd, keeping my eyes lowered, yet wondering what the hell I was doing in such a swishy place. I saw some local luminaries, Kay Ladoucer from city council, who also chaired several prominent charities. She was carrying on an animated conversation with Pierre Castille, the handsome billionaire land developer known for being a reclusive bachelor. He looked my way and I averted my eyes. Then I realized what he was actually looking at. Beside me were gathered several young and coltish daughters of Southern gentry, the kind of girls whose photographs you see in the *Times-Picayune* society pages.

The Smoking Time Jazz Club band was going to be playing tonight, but they hadn't yet taken the stage. I had heard them before at the Blue Nile. I loved the lead singer, a quirky girl with a partly shaved head and a powerful, hypnotic voice. But I wasn't here just to enjoy the music. Who was I meeting, and how would things unfold? Despite my nervousness, I could not avoid noticing a tall, attractive man talking with a long-legged woman wearing a brave red dress. As I watched (discreetly, I thought), he dismissed her and made his way over to me. All the air left my body as he blocked my path to the bar.

"Hello," he said, smiling. With his green eyes and blond hair he looked as though he'd stepped out of a magazine. He wore a beautifully tailored charcoal gray suit with a white shirt. His tie was thin and black. He seemed a little younger than the masseur, and more muscular too. I glanced over at the woman in the red dress, whose posture seemed to suggest defeat. He had left off talking to her to cross the room and greet *me*? Was he crazy?

"I'm . . . I'm Cassie," I said, hoping he couldn't sense my anxious thoughts.

"I see you don't have a drink. Let me get you one," he said, placing his hand on the small of my back and guiding me through the thickening crowd towards the bar.

"Oh. Yes. Why not?" The band was taking the stage. I could hear them warming up.

"What about your . . . companion?" I asked.

"What companion?" He seemed genuinely puzzled.

I glanced over my shoulder to where the woman had stood. She was gone.

He pulled out an empty stool at the bar and gestured for me to sit. Then he leaned towards me, moving a strand of hair behind my ear so that he could put his mouth close to it. I felt his warm breath. I couldn't help but close my eyes and lean into him.

"Cassie, I've ordered you some champagne," he said. "I'm going to check on something. While I'm away, I want you to do me a favor." He put a finger to my jawline and gently traced it. He was looking deep into my eyes. The man was beguiling, his beautiful mouth just an inch away from my own.

"While I'm gone, take off your panties. Drop them on the floor under the bar. But don't let anyone see."

"Here? Now?" I caught my reflection in the mirror over the bar and saw my eyebrows shoot up.

A wicked and perfect smile played across his mouth. Two days' worth of stubble didn't take away from his polish either.

I turned and watched him walk away, passing the bandstand and the pretty lead singer. I looked around at the oblivious crowd now craning to watch the band begin. The opening riffs were brassy and loud, the bass reverberating deep in my body. I looked towards the women's washroom. If I left my stool, I'd lose my place at the bar. Then he wouldn't find me.

The room was filling up. The lights were dimmed a bit more. A cold flute of champagne was placed in front of me. I was alone, at a bar, contemplating removing my underwear because a hot, young man had asked me to. What if I was caught? Surely I'd be thrown out for lewd behavior. I tried to remember what panties I had on. A black thong. Simple, silky. How to squirm out of panties in public, unnoticed, wasn't something I had learned at Girl Scouts.

I pulled the stool closer to the bar. Then, watching myself in the mirror, I did a practice run, moving my forearm and hand across my lap, while above the line of the bar my upper arm and shoulder appeared still. Good, it could work. I moved quickly, my hand under the bar gathering the front of my skirt. I slipped the other hand up my thigh, wrapping a finger through my thong and lifting my buttocks off the stool ever so slightly, hooking my heels into the base of the stool to get leverage. Just as I yanked hard, the song came to an abrupt end. I thought I was the only one to hear the rip, like a needle skipping across a record. But a man with a shaved head, who'd been standing with his back to me, turned to see what had made that sound. I froze. Oh no.

I smiled at him awkwardly and let out a nervous laugh. This man was riveting with crinkly eyes like Will's, but his were icy blue. He had on a black suit, with a black shirt and black tie. For a man who was probably closer to fifty than thirty, he had the lithe build of a soccer player.

Leaning towards me, he said, "Got them off yet?" He took in my expression of shock with a bemused smile, then took a sip of his scotch and plopped the empty glass down, wiping his mouth with the back of his wide hand. "Your panties, I mean. Are they off?" he said in a British accent.

I looked around in case anyone had heard him. But the music had started up again.

"Who are you?"

"The real question is, do you accept the Step?"

"The Step? What? You? I thought it was going to be with the other guy."

"I can assure you, Cassie, you're in good hands with me. Do you accept the Step?"

"What's going to happen?" Panicking, I looked around. But no one was watching us; they were watching the band.

No one cared what we were talking about either. It was as though we were invisible.

"What's going to happen?" I asked again.

"Everything you want, nothing you don't."

"Is that what you're all trained to say?" I said, with a hint of playfulness. I could do this. I could definitely do this with him. I yanked my thong again and this time the waistband cut across the tops of my thighs, leaving me in a deeply uncomfortable position.

"Do you accept the Step, Cassie? I can ask only three times," he said patiently. His eyes traveled down to my skirt.

"Maybe if I went to the ladies'—"

He turned and summoned the bartender.

"I'll take the bill, please, and put her champagne on it, would you?"

"Wait. Are you going?"

He smiled at me and pulled two twenties out of his money clip.

"Don't go," I said, lifting my arm from beneath the bar and placing it on his firm forearm. "I accept the Step."

"Good girl," he said, shoving his money clip back in his pocket.

He removed his dinner jacket and asked me to hold it in my lap. Standing beside me at the bar, he turned to the side, as if to watch the band. When he jolted my bar stool backwards a little, and my stomach took a second to catch up. He pressed himself against my back, his hot mouth next to my ear. I could feel his erection against the small of my back, where the first man had put his hand.

"Cassie, you look beautiful in that dress, but those panties need to come off, right now," he whispered hoarsely. "Because I'm going to play with you, if that's okay with you."

"Here? Now?" I swallowed.

"Oh yes."

"What if someone catches us?"

"No one will. I promise."

My back to his chest, both of us facing the band, he slipped his right hand under my skirt and followed the crevice between my thighs to my thong. With expert ease, he dipped a finger inside me. I was wet. This was crazy. The band kicked up the tempo and the singer's voice was like a musical instrument, her words pouring out at the exact moment that two of his fingers secured themselves around my thong's waistband.

"Lift, my love," he commanded, and with expert timing, he slid the damaged thong forward to my knees. I quickly shimmied it down to my ankles and let it fall discreetly to the floor. The place was dark, loud and crowded. Even if I screamed, it wouldn't cause a commotion.

I felt his hand slowly circle my inner thigh, teasing me just enough, as he continued to breathe into my ear. I imagined what we must look like: an affectionate couple watching the band. Only the two of us knew that his right hand was ravaging me. Secure that no one was watching, he got bolder and glided his other hand across my right breast, letting it linger there for a moment. Then he circled my breast with a wide palm until he could feel my nipple harden.

"I wish I could take this nipple in my mouth. But I can't because we're in a room full of people," he whispered in my ear. "Is this making you wetter?"

Oh God, it was. I nodded.

"If I slid my fingers inside you right now, would you still be wet?"

"Yes," I said.

"Promise?"

I nodded and then felt his other hand coming to life again under the jacket resting on my lap. It glided up my thighs, and then one finger parted me. This almost sent me toppling sideways, but he held me firmly. He nudged my right thigh open a little more, and I spread his jacket wider to conceal what was occurring beneath it.

"Take a sip of your champagne, Cassie," he said. I grabbed the cool glass, felt the burst of bubbles on my tongue. "I'm going to make you come right here."

Before I could even swallow, his fingers had begun to coax me open. The feel of it was so marvelous, I choked a little on my drink. No one standing near us could have known that the most delicious things were being done to me.

"Feel that, Cassie?" he whispered in that sexy accent. "Arch into me, baby," he said. "That's it."

My pelvis pushed down on his hand, now cupped beneath me. His fingers dipped in and out of me while his thumb traced circles around me. I closed my eyes. My entire body felt suspended in his strong hand, held as if in a swing.

"No one can see what I'm doing," he whispered. "Everyone thinks I'm talking to you about how much I love the band. Can you feel that?"

"Yes, oh God, yes."

He pressed himself into my back again. I leaned into this deliciousness, my right hand reaching up and cupping his working shoulder, my left arm holding the jacket steady. I felt his taut arm muscles as his thumb worked those magic circles, his deft fingers gliding in and out of me. He was playing me like an instrument. I lost myself in the darkness of the room, the beat of the music, the waves of pleasure. I wanted more of him inside me, not just fingers. Him. All of him. I edged my right thigh out and he read his cue to let his fingers explore deeper. I bent my head forward. I tried to look like I was totally lost in the music, but I was reeling with the swells this man was creating in my body, over and over, now building to a heavenly climax.

"Cassie, I can feel it. You're going to come in my hand, aren't you, girl?" he whispered.

I grabbed the bar with my right hand, feeling in a trance, and the room went black, the music mingling with a low moan (mine?) that had me bucking backwards. He was like a wall containing me as wave after wave flooded me. Oh sweet Jesus, I couldn't believe he could do this to me, right there. I couldn't believe I had just come in a loud, dark room full of strangers, some of them less than two feet away from me. He slowed his thumb as the waves in my body subsided; the room came into focus again. He stood still, holding me for a moment. When I shifted slightly, he pulled his fingers away gently, tracing them across my exposed thigh.

He slid my champagne glass in front of me. "You're fearless, Cassie."

I took the glass in my unsteady hand and gulped it down, then set the empty flute a little too loudly on the bar. I grinned and so did he. He was looking at me as if for the first time.

"You're gorgeous, you know that?" he said.

And instead of saying something self-deprecating, for once I believed it. "Thank you."

"Thank *you*," he said, signaling the bartender for the bill. He pulled off the two twenties again.

"Keep the change," he said to the bartender. Then he fished something out of his pocket. "And this is for you," he said, flicking what looked like a coin in the air and slapping it down on the bar.

When he lifted his palm, I saw my Step Two charm glowing under the bar lights, the word *Courage* engraved in script.

"It's been charming," he said, kissing my hair. Then he plucked his jacket off my lap and disappeared into the crowd.

After securing my charm and admiring it and its partner on my bracelet, I slid off the stool, my legs so rubbery beneath me I almost collapsed on the floor next to my abandoned thong. As I moved through the dark crowd, my breathing was still staggered, my sight blurry. I smacked right into a tiny girl in high platforms, nearly knocking her over. At first I didn't recognize Tracina, because she was all dolled up, her curly hair a wild corona, her brown skin contrasting dramatically with her lime-green dress. And I definitely didn't recognize Will in a smart dinner jacket and tie. He looked . . . sexy as hell.

"See?" she said, slapping Will hard across the chest. "I told Will it was you!"

Shit! This can't be happening. Not now. Not here.

"Hiiii" was all I could manage.

"As soon as I saw you and that . . . guy, I was like, 'Will, check out *Cassie* on a *date!*'" she said, snapping her fingers and singsonging that last word. She was swaying drunkenly.

Will looked twitchy and uncomfortable. Did they see me pressing into that man's stomach, grabbing his shoulder, writhing? Oh God! Could they tell what we were doing? Surely not. It was so dark, so loud. Where had they been standing? I was panic-stricken, yet there was nothing to do now but make small talk about the band. Then flee.

"Where'd he go?" Tracina asked.

"Who?"

"Your hot date?"

"Oh . . . he went to get the car. We're leaving. We have to go. Yeah . . . so—" I could feel sweat dripping down my cleavage and the back of my neck.

"But the band is going to play another set. These are tough tickets to get your hands on, Cassie."

"Maybe they've heard enough music for tonight," Will

said stiffly, taking a gulp of his beer. Was that jealousy I sensed? He could barely look at me. I had to get out of there.

"Well, I don't want to keep him waiting so . . . see you tomorrow," I mumbled, waving and already walking towards the elevators.

Holy hell. Inside the elevator, alone, I hopped up and down as though that would make it get to the ground floor faster. I had to get out and pull myself together. I let a stranger put his hands on me, *in* me—in public—and drive me half wild, while my boss and his girlfriend were standing somewhere nearby. What had they seen? How could something so marvelously sexy take such an ill turn? But I had to let it go for now. I'd talk to Matilda. She'd know what to do.

The elevator doors opened. I stepped out hurried through the lobby and out the glass doors to the street. It was a lovely night, the air refreshing. The limo was waiting exactly where it had dropped me off. I opened the back door before the driver could react, climbed in and sat down, still feeling the night air travel up my skirt, cooling the dampness between my thighs.

VI

Every May, the Spring Fling on Magazine Street high-lighted just how little Frenchmen Street had to offer in terms of daytime attractions. Five miles of shopping, music and pedestrian traffic drew crowds to the restaurants and cafés in the Lower Garden District. No such luck in Marigny. Frenchmen was a nighttime spot, where people came to listen to jazz and get drunk. Will's face said it all as he pored over the receipts from the previous day, the muscles in his forearms twitching as he punched in the figures on his aging adding machine.

"Why did my dad have to buy *this* building and put a daytime café on *this* street? And why did the Castilles have to build *that* condo right across from us?"

He let his pencil drop. It had been a bad month financially.

"Special delivery," I said, trying to lighten the mood. I pointed to the Americano on his desk that I'd freshly brewed for him. He didn't even look at it.

"What if we put a half-dozen tables in the back on my parking spot, string some patio lanterns, pipe in music and call it a patio? It might be pretty back there. Quieter," he said in a daze.

I could have been anyone standing there.

Just then, Tracina bounded into the office.

"If we're talking about renos, fix the toilets, the broken chairs and the goddamn floor tiles on the patio first, babe." She tossed her purse onto the chair in the corner. Then she whipped off her baggy white T-shirt in front of me and Will and changed into a tight red one she plucked out of her purse, the one she always wore on the night shift. She was so casual, so confident with her tiny, perfect body.

I tried to avert my eyes.

Spring Fling gave Will more gray hairs than losing business to Mardi Gras or the jazz festival. But gray hairs on Will only made him hotter. He was one of those guys who got better looking with age, something I had been about to say out loud that morning when Tracina interrupted. My two escapades and the boldness they were engendering in me had me blurting out all sorts of things. I was even swearing more, much to the consternation of poor Dell and her little red pocket Bible.

"Busy today?" Tracina asked, tucking in her T-shirt.

I was ending my shift just as she was beginning hers, with no tables to hand over. It was that dead.

"Not really."

"Not at all," said Will. "Spring Fling."

"Fuck Spring Fling," she said, prancing out of the room.

I watched her fluffy ponytail bob its way down the hall to the dining room.

"She's amazing," I said.

"That's one word for her," Will responded, dragging his fingers through his hair. He did that so often I wondered if there were trenches in his skull. Finally, he seemed to notice I was there. He looked up at me. "Plans tonight?"

"Nope."

"Not seeing that guy?"

"What guy?" I asked, perplexed.

"The guy from Halo."

"Oh *that* guy," I said, my heart speeding up. It'd been weeks since that night and neither he nor Tracina had brought it up, Tracina because she was probably too drunk to remember and Will because he never pried. Had he seen something after all?

"That guy was just a one-time date. There was no real chemistry."

Will squinted as though he remembered things a little differently. "No chemistry?" He turned back to his adding machine and punched in more numbers. "Could have fooled me."

When I asked Matilda what to do if I ever ran into someone I knew while out on a S.E.C.R.E.T. date, she told me that the truth was always better than a lie. And yet, here I was, lying.

"Will, Tracina's here, so I'm off. I'll see you tomorrow," I said, making ready to bolt.

"Cassie!" Will said, startling me.

Please don't ask me any more questions, I prayed silently.

Will met my eye. "Thanks for the coffee," he said.

I saluted and left.

"Cassie!"

What did he want this time? I turned and walked back to poke my head through the doorway.

"You looked really . . . good that night. Great, even."

"Oh. Well. Thanks," I said, no doubt blushing like a teen. Oh, Will. Poor Will. Poor Café Rose. Something had to be done soon.

It was inevitable. That evening Tracina got the heel of one of her neon pumps caught in a crack in the sidewalk. Her toes moved forward, but the heel stayed put, wrenching one of her bird-like ankles. She had warned—and had been warned—about the cracks in the pavement and the perils of wearing those pumps at work. But such is a woman's vanity, and such was my life, since I was the one who had to absorb a few of her night shifts until her puffed-up ankle returned to its normal dainty size. I complained to Matilda, who had asked me to keep her aware of my work schedule. I was hoping my next fantasy would take place in the Mansion, and I was also hoping it would happen soon. But it was looking more and more like this month might be fantasy-free. "Not a problem," she said. "We will just schedule two events next month." But still, memories of that interlude in the jazz bar were fading and the truth was, I was longing for more.

Thank goodness for Spring Fling was all I could think, while wiping down the tables. I couldn't have made it through a week of double shifts if we'd been busy. The days stayed dead quiet, but the early evenings cast an even sadder mood over our part of the city. There were so few customers to absorb the glow off the streetlights, it just bounced around the walls and glass, giving the Café the feel of a lonely painting. Will was staying at Tracina's to help her get around, so his reassuring presence wasn't felt upstairs. I didn't mind. I had a couple of good books on the go, and was even boldly using my free time to scribble some thoughts into my fantasy journal, which was the only homework S.E.C.R.E.T. had asked me to do.

That's actually what I was doing at the bar when the door chimes alerted me to what I thought was a late-night customer. But it was the pastry delivery man, odd because normally those guys made their drop at the crack of dawn, when Dell was around to sign off on the waybill. I had sent the cook home hours before, since the only things I'd serve after 7 p.m. were coffee and dessert, and only to people who were wrapping up their meal. I turned to watch as a young man in a gray hoodie pushing a dolly stacked with pastry boxes walked right up to me without saying a word.

"I'm sorry," I said, sliding off my stool and hiding my journal behind my back, "but aren't you a little late? Don't you normally come in the mor—"

He moved past me, removed his hoodie and shot me a smile over his shoulder. He had close-cropped hair, a chiseled face with dark blue eyes and forearms covered in tattoos. In my mind I saw a freeze-frame of every high school bad boy who'd made my heart ache.

"I'll just put these in the kitchen. Meet you there?" he said, holding up his clipboard.

I had a feeling I was going to receive a lot more than two-dozen beignets and a tray of Key lime tarts. Seconds after he punched open the doors to the darkened kitchen, I heard a crash that made me glad Will wasn't upstairs. And the cacophony didn't happen just once. It was in stages. First a crash, then a series of bangs, then another metallic nightmare.

"Oh my God!" I yelled, inching my way to the kitchen door, behind which I could hear groaning. "Are you okay?"

I shoved the door open and felt a body, his body, move a little. I felt along the inside wall and hit the fluorescent overheads, and there he was lying on the floor, clutching his ribs. Pastries of various pastel hues were smeared across the floor, leading to the walk-in fridge.

"I seriously screwed this up," he grunted.

I would have laughed, but my heart hadn't calmed down enough.

"Are you okay?" I asked again, gingerly approaching him like he was a dog that had been hit by a car and might run away if I moved too fast.

"I think so, yeah. Wow, sorry about the mess."

"Are you one of the guys from . . . you know?"

"Yeah. I'm supposed to "take you by surprise." Ta-da! Ow," he said, grabbing his elbow and collapsing back on the floor, a box of pecan pie his accidental pillow.

"Well, you did take me by surprise, in a way," I said, laughing at the mess he'd made. From the looks of it, his dolly had careened into Dell's steel-topped kitchen island, sending all the pots and pans suspended over it crashing to the floor.

"Want some help?" I asked, extending my hand. What a face. If a bad boy could also be angelic, he would look like this. He was twenty-eight, maybe thirty, tops. He had a slight Cajun accent, too, local and very sexy. He unzipped his hoodie, shrugged it off and whipped it across the floor to get a better look at his injured elbow. He was oblivious of the fact that he was revealing a boxer's torso under his white tank top, with intricate tattoos covering his arms and shoulders.

"That's going to be a really nice bruise tomorrow morning," he said, standing next to me.

He wasn't tall, but his sexy brutishness gave him incredible presence. After he shook off the last vestiges of pain, he stretched backwards, taking me in.

"Wow. You're really pretty," he said.

"I . . . think we have a first-aid kit or something around here."

As I walked past him towards the office, he grabbed me by the elbow and gently tugged me close to him.

"So? Will you?"

"Will I what?" I asked. Hazel. The eyes were definitely hazel.

"Will you do this Step with me?"

"That's not how you're supposed to say it."

"Damn," he said, racking his brain.

He was so cute, but not too swift, this one, which I suppose didn't matter.

"You're supposed to ask, 'Will you *accept* the Step?'"

"Right. Will you accept the Step?"

"Here? Now? With you?"

"Yeah. Here. Now. With me," he said, cocking his head, giving me a crooked smile. Despite his rough-hewn exterior, and a hairline scar on his upper lip, he had the whitest teeth I'd ever seen. "Are you going to make me beg?" he added. "Okay, then. Pretty please?"

I was enjoying this. A lot. And decided to play it out a little longer. "What are you going to do to me?"

"I know this one," he said. "I'm going to do everything you want, nothing you don't."

"Good answer."

"See? I don't totally suck." So sweet and so sexy. "So? Will you accept the Step?"

"Which one is it?"

"Uh . . . three, I think. *Trust?*"

"Right," I said, surveying the damage in the kitchen. "You come in here just as I'm closing and wreak the kind of havoc that's going to keep me here after hours cleaning up." I put my hands on my hips and squinted at him as though I had to really think about my choice. This was too much fun. "And do you really think you're in any shape to—"

"I don't get it. Are you saying you don't accept the Step?" He winced as though in real pain. "Fuck, I screwed up."

After a good, long pause, I said, "Nah. I'll . . . accept the Step."

"Wooo!" he said, clapping his hands hard, which sent me giggling. "I won't let you down, Cassie," he said, flicking off the fluorescent overheads, leaving us lit only by the warm glow of the streetlights streaming in through the kitchen cutout. He took a step back towards me and held my face in his hands.

In the end it wasn't the special late-night delivery or the accident that took me by surprise. It was *this*. This kiss. Suddenly he had me against the cool tile wall of the kitchen, his firm body pressing hard enough to let me know that he meant it; Jesus, I could feel him getting hard. A second later, my shirt was off and tossed on top of his hoodie on the floor. There had been no kissing the first two times and I hadn't missed it. But this, *this* was something else. My knees softened to the point where he had to move his hands to my waist to prevent me from collapsing to the floor. When had I *ever* been kissed like this, with just the right amount of urgency? Never in my life.

His tongue explored my mouth, with a need that matched my own. He tasted faintly like my favorite kind of cinnamon gum. After a few more seconds of deep kissing, he gently bit my bottom lip, and then his beautiful mouth moved from mine down the side of my neck, searching and kissing and finally landing on a spot just above my collarbone. He kissed me there, demandingly, which made me sigh. His hands seemed to pave the way for his mouth, so after they had freed my breasts from my bra, his mouth eagerly followed. His mouth traveled over one nipple until its hardness sent him searching for the other one, while he slipped a hand down the front of my jeans to discover what I had suspected was true: I was completely wet. He stopped kissing me and held my gaze while his fingers explored me, his eyes glassy and intense. Then he took his hand out of my pants and put a finger into his mouth. I thought I would come right then.

"I'm starving. Get these jeans off, will you? I'll set the table."

The feral look in his eyes, the layer of sweat sheening his perfect body, the hangdog smile. My God, this boy had me. I looked around at the creamy sweet carnage smeared all over the floor.

"Here? In the kitchen?" I asked, pulling my belt loose.

"Right here." And with a sweep of his tattooed arm, he cleared the rest of the debris off Dell's stainless steel table. The metal bowls, the pots and pans, the whisks and plastic utensils all went clattering to the floor. Then he grabbed a checkered tablecloth from the shelf beneath and flung it across the metal top. I stepped out of my jeans and stood there with my arms crossed over my nakedness.

"Know what's for dessert?" he said, turning to face me, an eyebrow cocked. "You."

He took a few steps towards me and enveloped me in his arms, kissing me again. Then he gently lifted me onto the table and left me there, legs dangling. I watched him walk over to the walk-in fridge and disappear inside.

"Let's see now . . ." he said. He emerged with an armful of containers and the whipped cream dispenser.

"What on earth are you doing?" I asked.

"Close your eyes and lie back."

And with that, he moved to my ankles, circled them with his hands and yanked me to the bottom edge of the table. Then he parted my legs with embarrassing ease. I let out a giggly scream that came to a stunned halt when he squirted whipped cream in the middle of my belly button. Then he squirted two dollops on each nipple and regarded his work earnestly.

"What are you doing!"

"Making dessert. I'm a pastry chef in real life, if you can believe it. Let's see . . . one more . . ." And with that, he drew a line of whipped cream from my belly button all the way down. Then he grabbed the container with the chocolate icing and gently dolloped some of that on me. He reached over and took a single maraschino cherry and placed it over my belly button. I tried to stop giggling but couldn't. It was all cold and ticklish and also incredibly hot. He gave his work a long look, then bent and closed his mouth over my belly button, took in the cherry and licked the cream clean off. Then he smeared the icing across my breasts, while his mouth made its eager descent. His sticky hands soon followed, crossing my torso, my stomach, then parting my legs. His tongue was hot and lush. At first he just lapped, not touching me directly, and I felt I would die if he didn't. Then, finally, he closed his mouth around me, moving it around and around, soft, hot, sticky, sending me into a narcotic haze. I felt his fingers tickle around the outside of me, their firmness complementing his soft, wet licks as he cleaned all the cream off me. I was aching for it like never before. He pulled me so quickly to the brink that I had to grasp the sides of the table to stabilize myself.

Then he stopped.

"Why are you stopping?" I gasped, breathless. I looked down at his hungry eyes, the back of his hand wiping the cream off his cheek.

"Cassie, could you feel what I was doing with my tongue?"

Um, yeah. I could *definitely* feel what he was doing. It was making me crazy.

"Yes," I said as calmly as I could.

"I want you to do that with your fingers. In front of me. *For* me."

"You want me to *what?*" I felt drunk as I looked at him, his face still adorably smeared with whipped cream.

"I want to watch you touch yourself," he said.

"But . . . I don't know how, really. I suck at it. I can get started, but then I feel . . . I don't know . . . and with you watching, I—"

"Give me your hand."

I reluctantly placed my hand in his. He held it firmly, guiding it to where I was hot and wet. He isolated my index finger. He placed it gently on me, and using his mouth there, he made me newly wet. His hand guided my finger in circles, his tongue darting around me. Oh God, it was incredible.

"I don't know what tastes better, you or the cream," he said.

Once I found the rhythm, he let go of my hand and my own fingers continued, while he gently moved his mouth over me. His hands grabbed the insides of my thighs, pressing them down into the table. He stopped for a second and watched me. I was on the very edge of ecstasy. I flung my head back, trying to take it all in, these sensations. He watched as I touched myself. Then his mouth soon joined my fingers.

"You feel that? You like that?" he said, between feverish licks.

"Oh yeah," I said, feeling every pulse and matching it with my own. I wasn't sure where the orgasm was building, but it was coming from someplace new, someplace deep, his wet tongue pulling something out of the very core of me. He pushed his fingers into me until they couldn't go any deeper, and as his other hand pressed my thighs open, pleasure ignited every fiber of my body. He sensed all the energy building inside me.

"Holy shit," I said, almost afraid of what was about to happen, like it was all going to be too much, and that's when the white hotness shot through me, forcing my hips higher, his cue to take over, pushing my hand away, kissing and licking me with vigor. The rush was so strong, it made me feel like I had to hold on to something, anything, for dear life.

"OhmyGodohmyGodohmyGod" was all I could muster, writhing on the slippery table, not caring if I crashed over

the side, dizzy with bliss. He clutched me, holding everything very still, until he could tell I was coming down off
from the precipice. And when my orgasm subsided, he
gently wiped his face on the inside of my thighs.

"That was . . . wow . . . really strong, Cassie. I could feel it."

"Yes. It was," I said, flinging my arm over my forehead
like I'd just woken from a dream.

"Wanna do it again?"

I laughed. "I don't think I'll ever be able to do that again."

He peeled himself off me, grabbed a couple of towels
from below the table and soaked them for a few seconds in
warm water at the sink by the fridge.

"Oh, you will."

"Where'd they find you?" I asked, slowly sitting up.

"Who?"

I let my legs dangle over the side of the table as he
returned to me and began gently cleaning the stickiness off
me with a warm towel. "The women from S.E.C.R.E.T."

"I'm not allowed to say, unless you become a member."

He brought the other towel to my face and hands. He
was thorough and gentle at the same time.

"Do you have kids?" I asked, out of nowhere.

There was a long pause. "I have . . . a son. We're doing
too much talking, Cassie."

I could totally picture his son, a little boy who looked
exactly like him but with bigger cheeks and no tattoos.

"Do they pay you to do this?"

He was wiping my arms, the towel turning over the soft

skin on my wrists. "'Course not. They don't need to pay me to do what I just did. I'd do that for you *any*time."

"So what's in it for you?"

He stopped then, my hand in the towel. He looked sternly into my face for a few seconds. "You really don't know, do you."

"Know what?"

"How beautiful you are."

I was speechless, my heart near to bursting. I had no choice but to believe him. He seemed so sincere. He finished wiping me and then tossed the dirty towels over his shoulder. He plucked his hoodie off the floor. He passed me my clothes and we both got dressed, mostly.

"Let me help you clean up," he said, kicking an empty garbage pail to the center of the room. It took us ten minutes to toss all the broken boxes, salvaging two. I filled a pail with hot water to wash the floor and I told him I could do the rest.

"Don't want to, but I gotta go now. Those are the rules. Thanks for dessert. And the cracked rib. And the broken elbow," he said, inching towards me. He hesitated at first, and then he stepped forward and placed a firm kiss on my lips.

"You're cool," he said.

"You're cool too," I said, surprised to hear myself say it out loud. "Will I see you again?"

"It's possible. But the odds are against me."

Then he backed out of the kitchen door, winked and left the Café. I watched him trot down the darkened street, the door chimes ringing goodbye.

I thought I had gotten rid of all the evidence. But there in the bright light of the next morning, I watched as Dell went over the stainless steel with a cloth and some special solvent. Maybe it was my imagination, but while she worked it was almost as if she was shooting me an admonishing look, one that said: *I don't know how a butt print got on my table, but I am not about to ask.*

I scanned the kitchen for my tray and, when I found it, bolted out the door to the dining room, only to run into another set of equally accusatorial eyes, this time Matilda's. She was sitting stock-still at table eight. I made my way towards her.

"What are you doing here?" I whispered, looking around.

"What do you mean, Cassie? This is one of my favorite cafés in New Orleans. Do you have a second to chat?"

"I *only* have a second," I said, lying, dropping a menu on the table. "It's been so busy. We've been down a waitress, and I've been working like a dog."

Truthfully, I was avoiding this conversation with Matilda because I was worried I'd broken the rules by talking to last night's man for too long and asking too many personal questions. I looked around the nearly empty restaurant. The breakfast crowd wouldn't hit for another half hour. Will was probably still at Tracina's, knowing I was scheduled for the breakfast shift. I slid into the chair, feeling guilty, but for what I didn't know.

"Did you have fun last night? With Jesse?" she asked.

"Jesse? That's his name?" Butterflies roused in my stomach.

"Yes. Jesse. First of all, I'm sorry if you were at all taken aback by his late arrival."

"It all worked out. Really well, actually," I said, looking down. "I . . . liked him."

"That's the other thing I'm here for. I think you've left an impression on him too, Cassie."

My heart leapt a little at the idea, and yet it was also flooded with the strange improbability of it all.

"Listen, it happens sometimes. People make a connection. Something clicks, and people want to know a little bit more about each other. So. What I can tell you is this: I can facilitate a meeting between you and Jesse. But if that's your choice, you'd be done. Your journey would end at Step Three. You'd be out of S.E.C.R.E.T. So would he."

I gulped.

"Truthfully," she added. "I didn't think Jesse is your type. I mean, he's sexy, but he's . . . ."

"Married?"

"Divorced. But I can't say anything more than that, Cassie. You think about it. I'll give you a week."

"Is he . . . Does he . . . want to see more of me?"

"Yes. He does," she said, a little sadly. "He's made that clear. Listen, Cassie. I can't tell you what to do, but I will say this: you're thriving. I can see it. I'd hate to see you stop this momentum for a man you know nothing about, so soon into your journey, based on one great night."

"Does it happen a lot?"

"Many women do end self-exploration prematurely. Most regret it. Not just in S.E.C.R.E.T. but in life."

Matilda placed her hand over mine, just as Will made his hurried way from the kitchen through the dining area, past us to where Tracina was attempting to parallel-park his truck in a small spot on the street in front of the restaurant. Even from where I was sitting, I could see it was a bad idea.

"Jesus! Stop! I told you to wait for me!" he yelled out the door.

I couldn't make out what Tracina said in reply, but it was loud and animated; the truck was askew and blocking traffic out front.

This is what it's like to have a boyfriend, I thought, and this is what it's like to be someone's girlfriend. You spend your days careening between bliss and disappointment, love and a bit of loathing, your every action weighed against the approval and disapproval of someone else. You don't own them and they don't own you, yet you're responsible for their every want and desire, some you can satisfy, some you never, ever will. Did I want that right now? Did I want to be some man's girlfriend? Did I even know anything about this man Jesse? A tattooed pastry chef who lives God-knows-where and has a kid? Sure, we had chemistry. But still. I hardly knew him!

Just as I was going over all of these things in my mind, outside the window I saw Tracina get out of the awkwardly parked truck and slam the door. I watched her as she dangled the keys in front of Will's face and then threw them at his feet.

Will picked up the keys and stood still for a few seconds, staring straight ahead.

"You know what?" I said, turning to Matilda once more. "I don't need any more time to think this through. I know what I want to do. I want more. I want S.E.C.R.E.T."

Matilda smiled. She gently placed my Step Three charm in my hand and patted it shut. "Jesse forgot to give this to you. But I think I'm the right person to offer it."

I looked at the word on the charm: *Trust*. Yes. But did I trust that I had made the right choice?

VII

Three weeks after my near resignation, my Step Four card arrived the old-fashioned way, by mail. I took the stairs back up to my apartment two at a time, feeling as excited to see those envelopes as I did contemplating the fantasies. It was like getting an invitation to an amazing party every month. Thoughts of Jesse would creep in now and again, mostly leaving me marveling that S.E.C.R.E.T. had picked him, a tattooed pastry chef, as my "type." But they were right. It made me realize that I'd chosen men, crushes, dates from such a narrow field. But I didn't regret my decision to stay in S.E.C.R.E.T. I was discovering too much about myself to stop now. Still, sometimes a memory of his arms, his wicked smile, would flash cross my mind and send a shiver through my whole body.

I ripped open the manila envelope. The smaller, more ornate one slipped out. My Step Four card. The word *Generosity* was elegantly printed on the back. Inside was an invitation for a home-cooked meal at the Mansion on the second Friday of the month. The Mansion. A home-cooked meal. Generosity indeed! The dress code, however, seemed weirdly specific: *Please wear black yoga pants, a plain white T-shirt, hair in a ponytail, sneakers, very little makeup.* A part of me was a little disappointed that I'd be going to the Mansion but wouldn't be allowed to wear something ultra-sexy or sophisticated. Oh well, at least I wouldn't have to go shopping beforehand. And at least I would finally be going to the Mansion, this mythical place that had seized my imagination in both good and slightly scary ways.

My thoughts were interrupted by a knock at the door. Will! I had promised him I would go with him to a restaurant supply auction in Metairie. We needed new trays, new chairs to replace the constantly fraying ones, and a sturdier prep table as ours had become mysteriously tippy. Will was also on the lookout for a dough mixer and a deep-fryer so we could start making our own pastries and maybe even beignets. Normally he would have asked Tracina to go with him, but her ankle was still on the mend. She didn't need crutches anymore, but she was nevertheless limping around the dining room, making Will feel guilty about the accident. She even jokingly suggested that had she not been dating him, she might have sued. I'm not sure she was kidding. I was to be Will's substitute girlfriend for the day.

"Be right there!" I yelled.

I shoved the envelope into my folder, slipped the folder between my mattresses and raced to the door, interrupting

Will's second knock. He had on one of the shirts I loved best on him, a muted red button-up that Tracina had bought. As much as she bugged me, I had to admit she was getting him to dress a lot better, had even convinced him to cut his hair a bit shorter.

"Hi! Right. Come in."

"I'm double-parked. Just come down when you're ready. You didn't hear my honking?"

"Sorry, no, I was . . . vacuuming."

Will glanced around my disheveled place, my unvacuumed living room. "Right," he said. "I'll be downstairs."

Will was distant and distracted on the short trip, changing the radio station whenever a song he didn't like came on, or if a good one was followed by a loud commercial.

"You seem jumpy," I said.

"I'm a little off, I guess."

"What's got you feeling off?"

"What do you care?"

"What do you mean 'what do you care'? I'm your friend. Thought I'd ask."

Will was silent for half a mile after that. I eventually turned away from him to take in the scenery. Finally, I couldn't take it anymore. "Are things with you and Tracina okay? I saw the little tiff over the car the other day."

"They're peachy, Cassie. Thank you for asking."

Whoa. I couldn't remember a time when Will had been so short with me. "Okay, then," I said. "I won't pry anymore. But if I knew you were going to be such crappy company today, I wouldn't have come. It's Sunday. My day off, remember? I thought this would be kind of fun, but—"

"I'm sorry," he interrupted. "You're not having *fun*? I should work a bit harder so you can have *fun*. Should I also stop interrupting your conversations with your new fun friends at work?"

He was talking about Matilda. I had asked her not to come by the restaurant so much, but the other day, after our talk about Jesse, Will had made a remark about how I shouldn't sit with customers when I'm working.

"She's a regular that I'm getting to know as a friend, is all. What is so wrong with that?"

"A regular customer who buys you jewelry to match her own?" He glanced over at the bracelet resting against my thigh. I loved its hammer finish, its pale gold sheen. It was so pretty, I couldn't help but wear it once I'd started to collect charms.

"This?" I said, holding up my wrist. "This. I . . . got it from a friend of hers. A friend of hers who makes them. I admired it and I wanted one too. That's what girls do, Will." I hoped I sounded convincing.

"How much did it cost? It looks like eighteen-karat gold."

"I saved for it. But that's really none of your business."

Will sighed and then went silent again.

"Am I not allowed to talk to our customers now, is that it? Because I gotta say, I work hard and that restaurant means a lot to me too. You know that I'd do anything to—"

"I'm sorry."

"—to—"

"*Listen* to me, Cassie. I am sorry. For real. I don't know why I'm so . . . Things are good with Tracina. But she's looking for . . . She wants to take things to the next level, and I'm not sure I'm ready, you know? So yes, I'm a little antsy. I'm a little on edge about things."

"Are you talking about *marriage?*" I nearly choked out the word. Why? I had rejected Will. Of course he should marry the girl he loves, right?

"No! God no. I mean like living together . . . but yeah, eventually marriage is what she wants."

"Is that what you want, Will?"

It was near high noon. The sun was pouring in through the sunroof, heating the tops of our heads. It was making me a little dizzy.

"Sure it is. I mean, why not, right? Why wouldn't I want that? She's a great gal," he said. He was looking straight ahead at the road. Then he turned to me for a moment, smiling weakly.

"Wow, your passion is blinding," I said, and we both laughed.

We arrived at the auction parking lot. It was half empty, and that was good—fewer people meant lower prices.

"Let's go buy some junk," he said, turning off the engine and almost jumping out of the car.

I had a momentary urge to sit there with him awhile, to comfort him, to touch his hair, to tell him it would be okay, that all he had to do was be honest with himself. But I also felt a pang of jealousy. Tracina had never seemed to mind my friendship with Will, wasn't the slightest bit suspicious of our time together, which I actually found a little galling. I knew I was no threat to her, and yet there was a part of me that wanted to cause some discomfort, a growing piece of me that wanted to prove I was a force to be reckoned with, even if just a small force.

But I didn't have a chance to say anything. Will was already halfway to the auction house, so I opened the car door, stepped out and followed him.

⁓

Friday came far too slowly. I had laid out a new pair of black yoga pants and a stretchy white T-shirt, which I decided to wear over a tight black tank top. Bad enough that I was wearing workout clothes, but I was careful to keep Dixie away from the pants. I didn't need to show up at the Mansion covered in furballs like some middle-aged cat lady. Right at the appointed time, I saw the limo pull up in front of my building. I was down and out the door before the driver could reach the buzzer.

"I'm here," I said, greeting him breathlessly.

With a gloved hand, he directed me to the car and opened the back door for me.

"Thank you," I said, settling into the plush seat and glancing back at my building. A lace curtain on the main floor parted and dropped. Poor confused Anna.

In the limo, there was a bucket with champagne and water on ice. I grabbed a water bottle; I did not want to arrive half-drunk. It was 7 p.m. and traffic was light, so we were in front of the S.E.C.R.E.T. headquarters in no time. Normally I took the gate off the street to the coach house, which was walled off from the main estate. This time the double gates leading directly to the Mansion opened automatically to allow the limo. Driving past the coach house, I could see over the wall of vines that all four dormer lights were on. I wondered what kind of work was being done in the coach house on a Friday night, what kinds of scenarios were being plotted for me and perhaps for other women who might also be going through the steps right now. Is there more than one? Am I the only one? So many questions I knew Matilda would never answer unless I became a S.E.C.R.E.T. member.

If the courtyard surrounding the coach house was a tangle of vines and bushes, the grounds of the Mansion beyond were trimmed and pristine, giving off an unearthly bright green glow that made the short grass look almost fake. There was a thick smell of roses in the air, roses that climbed halfway up the sides of the Mansion and looked like a giant crinoline in pink, yellow and white. The building had an Italianate facade typical of some of the grander homes in the neighborhood, with wide white columns that shaded the cool porch and supported a rounded balcony above. But it was grand in a way that the other houses in the area weren't. And though beautiful, it felt standoffish, a little too perfect. The whole building was covered in pale gray stucco with white cornices, and the porch wrapped around the top and bottom. Ornate Juliet balconies framed small doorways on the second and third floors. The whole place was lit from within by a warm, dusky glow that was inviting but also strange. We pulled up at the side entrance, but the cobblestone driveway continued over a rolling hill that led to a garage in the backyard. It looked like a place you'd never want to leave, but that you could never really live in either.

A woman dressed in a black-and-white uniform appeared from the side door. She waved. I lowered the limo's back window.

"You must be Cassie," she said. "My name is Claudette."

I'd become accustomed to waiting for the driver to get out of the car and open my door. When I stepped out, I noticed a few bodyguard types wandering the grounds, all wearing tailored suits and dark sunglasses, one of them speaking into an earpiece.

Claudette said, "He's waiting for you in the kitchen. He doesn't have very long, but he's quite excited to meet you."

"Who's *he*?" I asked, following her. And what did she mean by *he* doesn't have very long? Wasn't this supposed to be *my* fantasy? "You'll see," she said, keeping a reassuring hand on my back as she ushered me in through the door.

The side entrance had a marble floor in a black-and-white houndstooth design that carried down the hallway. A small fountain framed by two cherubs spilled water from vases into a shallow pool. Peonies poked out of giant vases. I caught a glimpse of a spectacular foyer to my right.

Another bodyguard was sitting on a chair at the base of the stairs, reading a newspaper.

"Why don't you wait outside," Claudette said to him.

The big man hesitated before abandoning the seat.

We made our way down a long hall, following the sound of loud hip-hop or rap music; I didn't really know the difference. My heart was pounding. I felt terribly underdressed for this place and wondered why they had me in such a plain, everyday outfit. The bodyguards, the tight schedule, the music—all was very confusing. We headed for what seemed to be the back of the house, passing a number of small plush chairs that lined a wide hallway, the music getting louder as we appraoched a set of double oak doors. I noticed the round inlaid windows were covered in black tissue paper. What was going on?

Claudette swung open a door and I was hit with the sound of music and the smell of warm soup, seafood, tomatoes, maybe, and spices. I turned to ask her where I was going and who I was going to meet, but she was gone, the door swinging quietly behind her. I looked around the large kitchen, decorated like an old-fashioned scullery, the shiny lacquer walls white to halfway up, then black. Dozens of stained copper pots were strung high over the kitchen island. The appliances were as big as small cars, but they were modern, only decked out to look old. The Sub-Zero fridge was like the one we had at work, except much newer and spotless. The stove was black iron, with eight burners, nothing like the one in the Café's kitchen. This was the kind of kitchen you'd find in a castle.

Then *he* popped up, in front of the stove, his shirtless back facing me. He had been bent over, adjusting a flame, and now he stirred something cooking in a big pot, all the while talking loudly into a phone receiver cradled in his neck. His back had the muscles of a natural athlete, not a bodybuilder; his brown skin was flawless. His baggy jeans were slung low but not too low, just enough to show off a ridiculously lean waist. He was talking and stirring at the same time.

"Excuse me?" I said, over the loud music, but not loud enough for him to turn around.

"I'm not saying I don't like the *whole* track," he was saying, "just that bridge. Listen." He waited for a beat to hit and held the phone into the air. "Hear that? I don't think it's the right sample. Did you ask him if I could hire Hep to pull it out for me? I know he's using him on his album, but this would be a personal favor."

He turned to face me, jumping a little at the fact that I'd been standing there and he hadn't known. He looked me over from head to toe, placing his free hand on his hip. His abs clenched. I tried not to stare, but it was difficult. This was perfection, this man. I glanced over my shoulder at the double oak doors. Still listening to the conversation on the phone, he gave me a smile that only people born with charisma to burn know how to give. It literally changed the temperature in the room. Then he held up a finger to signal *one more minute.* He looked familiar, that wide smile, those sleepy brown eyes.

"Tell him I'll pay him double to cut the single with me,"

he continued, the phone back at his neck, but now his eyes were on me, making me self-conscious all over again. Though not a big guy, he carried himself like he was a giant, almost as if he were famous or something, which of course he couldn't be. "We'll put him up at the Ritz. Has to be France. That's where we're cutting the album."

He covered the receiver and whispered, "Sorry. *One* minute. Make yourself comfortable, Cassie."

He knew my name! Then he continued, "I don't know. Maybe two days. I gotta see my granny in N.O. Then we go to New York, then France. The tour is in eight weeks, but I want to lay tracks for two singles. Release them while we're still on tour. I don't care. Tell him there's more where they came from. We're still doing that album."

Remembering to stir his pot again, he turned his back to me and tasted a little of the simmering dish. He seemed completely comfortable here, knowing exactly what drawer housed which utensil. With every pinch and stir, the muscles in his upper back and along his arms rippled and revealed themselves. The beat of the music was hypnotic, and every once in a while I'd see him get caught up in it, like it was taking him over and moving him from within. Still cradling the phone between his shoulder and his ear, he turned and stepped towards me, this time holding a spoonful of the soup, his other hand cupping beneath it.

"Just tasting my gran's recipe. Yeah. I'll bring you some. Now I'm gonna be busy for the next hour," he said, blowing on the spoon, then bringing it closer to my mouth.

I took a careful, hot bite. Gumbo. Oh God, better than Dell's, in fact, better than any I'd ever tasted.

"Make that two hours. I'll call you when I'm back at the hotel. Yup. Bye."

He dropped the spoon, hung up and turned to me. And he stood there like that, not saying a word, for at least ten seconds. He seemed totally confident, just standing like that, wordlessly, eyeing me up and down, the music still pumping. This man was someone. That was for sure. I decided to break the ice.

"I hope I wasn't interrupting anything important," I said over the music. He took a remote and aimed it over my head, lowering the volume. He didn't reply. I asked, "Who are you?"

He was about to say something, but just laughed and shook his head. "I'm whoever you want me to be, baby."

"But . . . those bodyguards out there. They're for you, right?"

And there it was again, that shake of the head, that shy boyish smile.

"No comment," he said. "We're not here to talk about me. We're here to talk about . . . what you got on. Tell me a little something about what it is you're wearing," he said, crossing his arms across his chest, then resting a thumb on his lips. He stepped out from behind the island and stood ten feet from me, assessing me like I was auditioning for something. My knees weakened at the sight of his belt buckle resting low in front. I tried not to stare, but this was a powerfully seductive man. I felt silly and old in my dumb yoga pants.

"Um, they asked me to wear this," I said, looking down at my idiotic sneakers.

"Nice. When I told them 'soccer mom,' I wasn't being literal. But I gotta say, this is pretty much what I had in mind. Just that the clothes are wrapped around a sexier package than I imagined."

"May I?" I asked, pointing to a stool at the island. I was shaking so much, if I didn't sit, I'd collapse.

"Sure. You like gumbo?" He grabbed his spoon and turned to the oven to give the pot another stir.

"I love it. It's . . . it's really delicious. Um . . . Are you going to *cook* for me? I'm just not sure I ever said anything about a fantasy involving cooking."

"I *am* going to cook for you. And you're going to do something for me," he said, pointing his spoon at me.

"I am?"

"You are."

"I thought this was *my* fantasy?"

"Are we gonna have a problem?" he asked, with a kind of cocksuredness that made me a little weak. He didn't seem like a man used to hearing the word *no*.

"Are you going to tell me your name?" I asked, feeling bolder.

"I use a different name for my work, but my real name is Shawn."

He turned the heat off and came around the kitchen island to stand beside me, towering over my little red stool. His hair was shorn close to his head. His right wrist held a riot of leather bracelets, rubber bands, and a gold chain that was thicker and shinier than mine. No charms. I caught a hint of musk off his skin, something that came from an expensive bottle.

I clenched my jaw. His boldness seemed to bring out something in me, something new and fierce. "Are you going to tell me who you are?"

"That's for you to figure out. Later. Right now, what I am to you is your sex-with-someone-famous fantasy. But this is S.E.C.R.E.T., remember? These things tend to work both ways, as I'm sure you're discovering. So, do you accept the Step?"

"Do you mean my fantasy is actually yours somehow too?"

"Yup."

"And I have to take it on your word that you're famous?"

"That's right." He placed one strong arm on the bar stool where I was sitting, right between my yoga-clad legs.

"Okay. I get that. But how on earth could I possibly be *your* fantasy."

As he spoke, he ran a firm finger up and down my thigh. Shivers darted right through me. "Cassie," he said, meeting my eyes, "when you're famous, everyone wants a piece of you, and *only* because you're famous. You asked for a fantasy with a famous person, but you didn't say they had to be famous *to you*. I said I'd do it if it was with someone who didn't know who the hell I was, like some anonymous soccer mom type, I said. Someone too busy shuffling her kids around to bother wearing anything but yoga pants and T-shirts. 'Cause I'm sick of show ponies. Know what I'm saying?"

"Soccer mom. So that's what I'm supposed to be?" I started to laugh then, and so did he. "Have you done this before? With S.E.C.R.E.T.?"

He ignored the question, making his way back to the oven range behind me to check on something baking inside.

"Looking good. Corn bread."

He shut the door. A moment later, he was behind me, inches away. He placed his hands on my shoulders and moved them slowly down my arms. I felt my pulse quicken as he gently gathered my hands behind my back and held my wrists together with one hand. I could feel his breath on my ear.

"Will you accept the Step, my little soccer mom?" he asked, reaching a hand up to my ponytail, sliding out the band holding back my hair, his mouth breathing into it as it cascaded down my shoulders.

"Yes," I managed to say, giggling. Soccer mom is a fantasy? Who knew?

"Good."

Then he moved his mouth closer to my ear. "Wanna know who I am?"

I nodded. He whispered his name, his work name, his "stage" name. I was glad that he wasn't facing me because my eyes bugged out. I wasn't into hip-hop music, but even I knew this stage name. And now, Shawn was sliding his hands up my T-shirt. He lifted it off as though it was made of gossamer. He reached around and touched my breasts through my tight Lycra top.

"This has to go too. Arms up!"

He stretched my yoga top over my head, and flung it across the kitchen. Then he grabbed my stool and spun me around to face him. He pulled me close to him so my knees were between his spread thighs, his right hand tilting my head up to face him, his left fingering my nipple. He tentatively slipped a thumb into my mouth and I instinctively sucked the lingering spices from the soup off it, which made him close his eyes. I liked how that seemed to make him go weak with want, made him sway a little. I sucked a little more forcefully.

"I bet you're good at it," he said, opening eyes heavy with pleasure. "I bet you can make a man die a little with that mouth of yours."

I stopped what I was doing. So far all my fantasies had involved me receiving pleasure, not giving any back. Now I wanted very badly to give, to be generous, as the Step demanded, but I didn't know a whole lot about how.

"I want to do something for you," I said.

"What's that, Cassie?" he asked, biting his bottom lip in agony as I closed my mouth around his index finger this time.

I gazed up into his eyes, my mouth closed around his finger for a second. Then with all the boldness I could muster, I said, "I want you in . . . my mouth. All of you."

The air gathered in my lungs but wouldn't release. I had actually said that. I had actually told a man, a very famous one, that I wanted to . . . give him a blowjob. Now what?

I had given exactly one blowjob in high school. I'd tried it with Scott a few times when he was drunk and demanded it, but it had been a horrible experience, ending in a sore jaw for me and Scott falling asleep. I didn't enjoy it. The prospect of trying this now—and failing—made me nervous. But as long as I was living out a sexual fantasy with a famous person, I decided to let the famous person do what famous people are good at: he would have to demand a certain level of service.

"I want you to show me how to . . . please you," I said.

He trailed his wet finger down my neck, and then, cupping my chin in his hand, he said, "I think I can do that."

This godly man wanted me to give him a blowjob!

"It's just . . . I don't know if I'm any good at it. I mean, if this is *your* fantasy, then it's going to suck, I'm afraid." It took me a second to realize what I had said that had made him laugh out loud. "I mean, suck in a *bad* way. That's what I mean."

He stopped laughing and I swear I felt that I could have fallen into his deep, black eyes, they were so intense. I could see why he was famous, without even being familiar with his music. He had charisma, presence, confidence.

At my request for lessons, he began.

"Let's start with getting you naked."

I stood and took a step back. As he watched, I slipped off the rest of my clothes, kicking off the sneakers, then sliding down the yoga pants, then my panties. He watched me. He wanted this. He wanted *me*. Me! I could feel it. In my mind I kept saying, *Go with it, go with this, he will show you, you will be okay.* My nerves were on my side as I fell under his delicious spell. He turned and pulled a chair out from the kitchen table and took a seat.

"You can't really screw up, Cassie, unless you bring your teeth into the mix. They're not invited. Anything else and you're going to make me a happy man. Come here."

I took a step towards him. Then another one. I was standing directly over him, naked. Taking my wrists in his large hands, he tugged me down to my knees in front of him. He smelled warm and spicy, or maybe it was the stew and the bread, but we were both getting hotter. He took my hands and placed them on his chest, then dragged them over his impossibly taut stomach.

"Undo my pants, Cassie."

Something inside me melted, and I reached down and unfastened his belt. He shuffled his pants to the floor. He was hard and big. And thick.

"Jesus," I whispered, wrapping my hands around him, feeling his soft skin. How could he be so . . . hard and so soft at the same time?

"Now lean in and kiss the tip," he said. "That's it, go slow at first. Like that, yeah. Kiss it. That's right."

I took him in my mouth and licked from the top to the base of his shaft, feeling his body rock as my mouth and hands developed a steady rhythm.

"That's right, just a little faster."

I quickened the pace as he gently moved one of my hands around him and left it there. I took him deep into my mouth even as my other hand reached under him.

"Yeah," he said, moving his fingers tenderly through my hair. "You got it. That's right."

My hands met my lips and I formed a vacuum around him, my whole mouth consuming him. I released him then, licking just his tip with the end of my tongue. He looked down at me as I looked up, and our eyes met. His face was blissful and relaxed, which sent a surge of power through my body. I had him. He was mine. I took him in my mouth again, sucking and pulling him into me, and felt a vibration in his pelvis. This made me even bolder, and I took more of him in my mouth. I could feel him pressing into me, yet at the same time, I felt him weakening, melting. I was doing this *to* him. I was in control, in charge. Any minute now, I was going to make this man come . . . in my mouth.

"Girl, you don't need my help."

The more I pleased him, the wetter I seemed to get, something that had never happened to me before. Why had I once seen this as a chore? My hand reached around behind him to clutch at his back, while my mouth pulled him deeper and deeper. Then, reading his body, I felt him hitting a tipping point and I slowed my rhythm.

"Ah, yeah, it's perfect. Don't stop!"

His words fueled my hunger. I took him deeper into my mouth, which made him clutch the counter for stability. When I looked up at his face and saw he was on the verge of coming on my command, I felt more empowered and even sexier.

"Oh, Cassie," he pleaded, my hair entwined in one of his hands, the other keeping his balance on the stool above me.

"Mother of God," he whispered, as I felt myself pulling the orgasm right out of him. He drew a sharp breath and stiffened. Then he went beautifully silent. After a few moments I felt him receding, and eventually sliding out of my mouth. I kissed that lovely place where his torso met his thighs. Then I grabbed my T-shirt from the floor and gently wiped my mouth. A feeling of triumph surged through me, and I smiled up at him.

"Man alive, girl," he gasped, stepping back from me. "You didn't need *any* instructions. That was . . . amazing."

"Really?" I said, stepping up to him. We were chest to chest, and I could feel the muscles of his chest against me.

"Really," he said, touching his forehead to mine. "A. Maze. Ing."

He had an astonished look on his face, and he was still breathing heavily. I was totally naked and standing on my clothes. I looked down.

"Pretty fucking adorable. There's a washroom behind the pantry there," he said, pointing.

I gathered my soccer mom uniform from the floor and began to walk away.

"Wait."

I turned, and he stepped towards me and planted a long, firm kiss on my mouth. "That was exactly what I needed," he said.

In the washroom I shut the door behind me. Even this small room off the pantry was lush and ornate, with gold taps and gold-velvet embossed wallpaper with burgundy paisley. The sink's pedestal was a woman's arms flowering out into hands that became the basin. I splashed cold water on my face and around the back of my neck. I took a mouthful of water and swallowed. Water dripped down my chest and into my cleavage. I traced it with my fingers. I had given someone pleasure, been generous, for the sake of doing it—and for no other reason.

I had begun to dress, when I heard a gentle knock on the door.

"It's me, open up."

Maybe unlike the masseur, Shawn wanted to say good-bye. I opened the door a crack. He eased his body into the washroom, and I felt my pulse speed up. He turned me around so that I was facing the mirror and he was behind me. Then he buried his head in the crook of my neck as he had done in the kitchen.

"This is for you," he said.

He had put his jeans back on, but I could feel him hard again behind me. And as I reached my arms up and around the back of his neck, I felt his pelvis press against me, the cool ceramic rim of the vanity on my thighs. I was wet in an instant. He bit into my neck gently and then slipped one arm forward and between my thighs. My back arched into his hand. I bent forward, closer to the mirror, and watched his reflection, his eyes closed, his hands moving down across my breasts, my stomach, his fingers fanning out. Even this had a rhythm for him, like he was finding a strain of music in my body. He was playing me, pulling me closer and closer, his fingers pulsing intensely inside me. To feel wanted, to be taken and touched like this, it was like coming to life from the inside out. My eyes met his in the mirror. The next thing I knew, everything was a blur of color and rhythm, and I felt myself explode into his hands, the heat rushing through me, and then the flood of relief.

"There it is, there it is," he cooed, and without realizing it, I was pushing back on him until we both reached the wall behind us, leaning against it to stay upright. Then, for no real reason, I began to laugh.

"Thank you," I said, still out of breath. I remembered my clothes, the reason I'd come to the washroom to begin with. My soccer mom apparel was in a little pile on the floor in front of the vanity.

"Guess you have to put those back on," he said.

"I think so."

And after planting one more kiss on my neck, he backed out the door and shut it behind himself. My face in the mirror was flushed with air and life. I finished dressing, then splashed more water on my face.

"You are doing this," I whispered, smiling at myself in the mirror. "You *did* this. You just gave a blowjob to a musical heartthrob, billboard topper, Grammy winner. And then he just made you come in a bathroom." At that thought, I quietly squealed into my fists. *Ahhh!*

Fully dressed once again, my hair a sex-tossed mess, I re-entered the dim kitchen. The music was off. The pot was gone. So was the man. On the edge of the island was a small

Tupperware container with warm gumbo, a gold charm perched on top. I sat down on the bar stool and just breathed and thought about what had happened.

A few moments later, Claudette came through the door.

"Cassie, your limo's waiting. I hope you had a lovely stay with us," she said with a slight New Orleans drawl.

"Thank you, I did." I clutched the charm to my chest, grabbed my Tupperware container and was whisked out the side door of the Mansion and into the plush leather seat of the limo.

As we drove along Magazine Street, I took in the scenery outside but was really looking inward. I gripped the gold charm in the palm of my hand. Why had I always been afraid of giving? What was my fear about? Feeling used, probably. Feeling like giving would deplete me. But giving actually gave me satisfaction; it gave me pleasure to please. I rolled down the window and let the wind cool my face while the gumbo warmed my lap. This was the point of S.E.C.R.E.T., to get us to surrender the body to its needs entirely, and to help others surrender too. Why had that seemed so difficult before? I opened my palm and looked at the glowing gold charm, the word *Generosity*, engraved in elegant script.

"Indeed," I said out loud, as I secured the fourth charm to my bracelet.

VIII

Summer covered the city like a thick wool blanket. And since the Café's air-conditioning was always challenged, the only relief from the heat was a brief visit to the walk-in refrigerator. Tracina, Dell and I covered for each other as we did it, careful not to let Will see us waste the cold air.

"Just move slower," Will advised one day. "That's what they did in the olden days."

"Shouldn't be a problem for Dell," Tracina snarked, while unloading a bin of dirty dishes next to me.

I wanted to blame the heat for her mood, but there was no real correlation. A track by my new favorite hip-hop artist came on the radio and I turned up the volume, sending Tracina into a tizzy.

"Why's a white girl listening to this beautiful black man's music?" she asked, turning the volume down.

"I'm a fan."

"A fan? You?"

"Actually, I'm quite familiar with his work," I said, barely concealing a smile. Tracina shook her head and walked away. I cheerfully turned up the volume and continued bleaching the cutting boards. Though I could never imagine myself in a sea of fans at his feet, the thrill of that fantasy had lingered. I'd get a memory flash of my skin against his, his face tightened in ecstasy, and a shiver of arousal would snake up my spine. It was one thing to use a fantasy to trigger that feeling, and an entirely different thing when that fantasy was realized, stored and then recalled. This was what made S.E.C.R.E.T. so marvelous. These fantasies were creating sense memories that I could store for life and have at the ready whenever I needed a boost. I was not a voyeur. I was a participant.

But despite these thrilling scenarios, I had begun to fantasize about a certain kind of sex that had so far eluded me. I wanted . . . well, I wanted a man inside me. *There.* Admitting to myself that I wanted something was getting easier.

The hard part was admitting it out loud to Matilda, who later that day sat across from me at Tracey's on Magazine Street. It had become our regular place, and not just because it was down the street from the Mansion. Its raucous sports bar atmosphere made it easier to talk without anyone overhearing.

I told myself today was the day I would ask her why none of the men had wanted to do it with me. My brain, of course, had interpreted it as rejection, leftover fears from my days with Scott. He had a knack for making me feel unwanted. And because I was beginning to understand the weird reciprocity at work with the fantasies, I started to worry that perhaps I was not fulfilling the men I was with—that I was, in a word, undesirable.

"Nonsense, Cassie! You are very desirable!" Matilda said a little too loudly during a sudden gap in the music. In a whisper, she added, "Are you saying you're unhappy with your scenarios?"

"No! I have zero complaints about the fantasies so far," I said. "In fact, they amaze me. But why has no one wanted to . . . *you know?*"

"Cassie, there's a reason these fantasies haven't involved full-on sex," she said. "Sometimes sex has a way of turning into love for some women. Their emotions get caught up with the ecstasy and they forget that physical pleasure and love can be two separate things. We're not trying to help you fall in love with a man. You clearly don't need help doing that. We want you to fall in love with yourself first. After that, you'll be in a much better position to choose a partner, the right one. A *real* one."

"So you're saying I can't have sex in my fantasies because you're afraid I'll fall in love?"

"No. What I mean is we need to wait until you understand the tricks your body will play on your mind. Sex creates chemicals that can be mistaken for love. Not understanding that about our bodies creates a lot of misunderstanding and unnecessary suffering."

"I see," I said, looking around the bar, one mostly filled with men having beers with other men. Fat, short, young or old, I used to wonder how they did it, how some men could have sex and then so easily disengage. I guess it wasn't their fault. It was chemical. Still, Matilda was right. I got attached easily. I ended up marrying the first man I had sex with because my entire body said it was the right thing, the *only* thing to do, even though my mind knew it was completely wrong. In fact, I almost got off the train at the Jesse stop because he talked to me, made me laugh and was an amazing kisser.

"Cassie, please don't worry so much. But believe me when I say to you that this is about sex. Pleasure and sex. Love, my dear, is a whole other thing."

My next fantasy card arrived almost six excruciating weeks later, after the heat wave had been replaced by a storm watch, the weather perfectly mirroring my frustration. The fantasies would take place over the course of a year, I was reminded. And though the Committee tried to space them out evenly, even Matilda admitted in a quick phone call that six weeks was unusual. "Patience, Cassie. You can't rush some things."

A few days later, at night, a courier rang the buzzer downstairs. I practically ran down the stairs to sign for what he had. I was so excited I almost kissed him on the mouth.

"I saw that you were up," he said, pointing to the dormers on the third floor of the Spinster Hotel. He was young, maybe twenty-five, with the kind of body only the most aggressive of bike couriers can achieve in a city this flat. But he was so damn cute that inviting him up crossed my mind.

"Thank you," I said, snatching the envelope from his sinewy hands. The wind whipped my hair around my face and sent my robe flapping up my legs.

"Oh, there's this too," he said, handing me a cushioned envelope the size of a small pillow. "Storm's coming. Dress appropriately," he added, taking one bold look at my legs and spinning away with a wave.

I took the stairs in twos, ripping open the card as I ran. It said: Step Five, *Fearlessness,* which sent a little chill down my spine. The card also said a limo was fetching me first thing in the morning, and that "appropriate attire is included."

As the wind rattled my windows that evening, I felt grateful that Scott and I had arrived a year after Hurricane Katrina and her sisters, Wilma and Rita, ravaged the city. Except for Isaac and a couple of other tropical storms that bent the trees and shattered some glass, there hadn't been a huge disaster on the scale of those hurricanes since, something this Michigan girl was grateful for. I was prepared for wet weather, but not the dangerous kind that sometimes happened down here.

I sliced open the pillowed envelope and spilled its contents on my bed. An outfit for tomorrow had been selected for me: a pair of tight white capris, a pale blue silken tunic cut low, a white scarf, black Jackie O–style glasses, and heeled espadrilles, all of which of course fit beautifully.

The next morning, I kept the limo waiting as I tried knotting the scarf different ways around my neck, eventually settling on wearing it as a kerchief. A glance in the mirror and I had to admit I looked a bit aristocratic. Even Dixie, who stretched out at my feet, seemed to give her approval. But I'll never forget the look on Anna's face, a Bayou woman born and bred, as I plucked a collapsible black umbrella from the stand in the foyer.

"If it storms, you'd be better off using an umbrella that comes on a fancy drink," she huffed.

I wondered if I should say something to her, make up a rich boyfriend, just to stop the curiosity about the limo from brewing into something bigger and less benign. Not today, I decided. No time.

"'Morning, Cassie," said the driver, holding open the door.

"Good morning," I said, trying not to sound too accustomed to being picked up by a long black limousine in the middle of Marigny.

"You won't be needing that where I'm taking you," he said, nodding towards my little umbrella. "We're leaving this gray weather behind."

How exciting, I thought. The traffic was sparse that morning, and if there was any, it seemed to be heading away from the lake we were driving towards. Near Pontchartrain Beach we kept right and drove past South Shore Harbor, hugging the violent shore, which, from time to time, I could make out between construction gaps on the dam. The water was choppy and angry, even though not a drop of rain had fallen. At Paris Road, the driver stayed left, moving along the bumpy gravel road and keeping the lagoon on our right.

Five minutes later, we made another right down yet another gravel road. I clutched the leather seat, fear creeping up on me. We came to a clearing in the brush, where the propeller of a dark-blue helicopter was making slow, ominous circles before speeding up.

"Um. Is that a helicopter?" A stupid question, the better one being: *Do you expect me to go up in that thing?* But the second question was lodged in my throat.

"You're going on a very special trip."

Am I? He clearly didn't know me very well. The idea of my getting into a helicopter was ludicrous, no matter what promises lay beyond the ride. The limo came to a full stop twenty feet from the helipad. This was not good at all. The driver stepped out and opened my door. I sat frozen in my seat, the word *no* emanating from every pore of my body.

"Cassie, there is nothing to be afraid of," the driver yelled over the loud wind and the even louder propeller. "Please follow that young man! He will take very good care of you! I promise!"

It was then that I noticed the pilot, who was holding his cap and running towards the limo. As he got closer, he combed back his sun-bleached blond hair with his fingers and placed the cap on his head, giving me the impression he rarely wore it otherwise. He saluted me in a sweetly awkward way.

"Cassie, I'm Captain Archer. I'm meant take you to your destination. Please come with me!" He must have seen me hesitate. "It's going to be fine."

What choice did I have? I suppose a few, including one to remain welded to the seat and demand that the driver take me home. Instead I launched myself out of the limo before my brain could convince me to do otherwise. Captain Archer clasped my wrist with a big tanned hand and we made a run for it, ducking under the speedy propeller.

In the helicopter, that same hand reached across my lap, brushing my thighs while he secured me in the back seat. *It's okay, it's okay, it's okay,* I kept telling myself over and over again. *There's nothing to be afraid of.* I felt the lash of stray hairs on my cheek and was grateful for my kerchief. As he carefully placed large headphones over my ears, I could smell mint gum on his breath. Then he looked at me with eyes that were deep gray and intense.

"Can you hear me?" he asked, his voice now buzzing directly in my ears through his microphone. Was that an Australian accent?

I nodded.

"I've got you, Cassie, don't worry. You're safe. Relax and enjoy the ride."

I did find it a little unnerving that S.E.C.R.E.T. participants all seemed to know my name. *This is my life,* I thought kind of headily. *A limo picks me up. No big thing. Makes its way to a waiting helicopter. Whatever. And an impossibly handsome pilot whisks me away to parts unknown.*

We lifted off and once we were above the ominous dark clouds, the day looked completely different, like one in a tropical paradise. Captain Archer caught me staring down at the clouds as we left the bad weather below us and angled towards the sunrise.

"That's a big storm brewing. But where we're going it won't touch us."

"Where *are* we going?"

"You'll see," he said, his eyes smiling, lingering on mine.

My butterflies were still there, but they were becoming more manageable, and the fear, something I could push through. That I would willingly head off in a helicopter when a storm was brewing, flying above it to who knows where, to do who knows what with who knows who, would have been impossible to imagine five months ago. But today, beneath the natural fear was a feeling I recognized as sheer excitement.

Once we had stabilized above the clouds, the helicopter sped towards the vivid blue Gulf. I alternated between watching the water below and watching the pilot's sculpted hands flicking this and that button with efficiency and ease. His forearms were tanned and lightly furred with pale blond hair. Was he going to be the one? Was he part of my fantasy? If so, we were off to a solid start.

"Where are we going?" I yelled, pulling off my scarf and letting my hair cascade. I was flirting. For the first time in my life, it seemed to come naturally.

"You'll see. It won't be long now!" he said with a wink.

I held his gaze, this time letting him be the one to break it first. I'd never done *that* before and it was a little intoxicating, flirting through my fear.

A few minutes later, I felt the helicopter begin to descend. Panic crept in. I couldn't see directly below us, so from my back-seat vantage point we looked to be landing directly in the blue Gulf waters. When the helicopter skids hit something solid, I realized we'd landed on a boat. It was a very big boat. In fact, a yacht.

The pilot hopped down and opened my door, offering me a hand.

I leapt onto the polished landing deck, shielding my eyes from the now-blinding sun and thinking how quickly weather can change.

"This is unbelievable," I said.

"It is," said the pilot, giving me the impression he might not have been referring to the boat. "I have been instructed to bring you here, and now I must leave."

"That's too bad," I said, meaning it. From the upper deck, I could look around. It was a yacht, indeed, and one of the most beautiful vehicles of any kind I'd ever seen in my life. The deck was gleaming, polished wood, the hull and the walls a vivid white. "Can you stay for a drink? Just one?"

What was I doing? The fantasies usually unfolded before me, and now I was interfering with whatever was planned for me. But the helicopter trip had energized me, and I wanted to continue the flirtation.

"I supposed one drink wouldn't hurt," he said. "Join me in the pool?"

Pool? My breath stopped when I leaned around the bow and saw the oval-shaped pool, *on a yacht,* circling the deck in front. White lounge chairs lined both sides, red-and-white striped towels casually folded over their backs. *For me? Was this all for me?* Whatever happens to me here doesn't matter, I thought, so long as I get to *swim*, in a *pool*, on a *yacht!* And though the waters were starting to get a bit choppy, the boat was huge and felt rock-solid, even with a small helicopter perched on top. It dawned on me that a bathing suit wasn't among the clothes provided, but the pilot was already making his way to the pool, dropping pieces of his clothing before turning the corner and disappearing from sight.

I waited a beat, then followed him. No one else seemed to be aboard the boat, the windows to the pilot's bay so darkly tinted you couldn't see the crew inside, if they were there. By the time I reached him poolside, the pilot was submerged, and by the look of the pile of clothes he'd left behind, he was naked.

"Get in. It's warm."

"Will you get in trouble?" I asked, feeling shy.

"Not unless you protest my being here."

"I won't do that," I said. "But . . . would you mind turning around?"

"I don't mind at all," he said, facing the other way. He was tanned all over, though I could see that his butt below the surface of the water was shining white. I hesitated for a moment, and then shook off the remnants of fear. I was in charge of this fantasy, it seemed, and no one was stopping me. I slipped out of my clothes, then carefully laid them across a lounge chair. I eased into the water, which felt warmer because there was a slight chill in the air, the kind of chill storms bring. The sun still shone hot, but there were dark clouds on the horizon and a feeling of electricity in the atmosphere.

"Okay, you can turn around now," I said, keeping my arms across my breasts, which were below the water. Why was I so shy? I also realized he hadn't asked me to accept the Step, which had become almost Pavlovian to me. After uttering those words, I slipped into a kind of trance that allowed me to go along with a fantasy. This time, *I* was the one propelling things forward with a man not already earmarked, though he should have been. I had never been one for blonds, but he was so masculine, his brown arms reaching for me, pulling me towards him through the water's resistance.

"Your skin feels amazing in the water," he said, running his hands down my back, lifting me onto his lap. I felt him stiffen. He bent to take one of my nipples boldly into his mouth, and his hand squeezed my naked buttocks. Our bodies splashed against each other as the pool water got choppier and choppier with our movements. At least that's what I thought was making the waves. I opened my eyes to the sky again and this time it cast a very different glow, a more malevolent one. The sun was obscured by indigo clouds, the kind that caused Captain Archer to stop nibbling at my shoulder.

"Oh jeez, that's a bad, bad sky," he said, standing up, toppling me from his lap. "I have to get that helicopter off the boat or it'll get tossed into the Gulf. You, my dear, are going below deck and you're not to move until someone comes to get you, do you hear me? This was really not in the plans. I'm sorry for that. I'll radio for some backup."

He was out of the pool in a second. There was no time for vanity. He held up a towel that swallowed me whole and placed my clothes in my hand. The wind whipped up a frenzy, nearly taking us both over the side. He grabbed me and pressed me against the wall of the bow, plucking a lifejacket off a hook above me.

"Go below, change, and put this jacket on!"

"Can't I go with you?" I said, fear gathering in my gut again. I clutched the towel under my chin and padded after him, dripping the whole way to the helipad.

"Too dangerous, Cassie. You're better off on this boat. It moves fast. It'll take you from the storm. Go below now and don't leave until someone comes to get you. And don't fret," he said, pressing a kiss to my forehead.

"But does anyone know I'm here?"

"Don't worry, all is well, my dear!"

I pulled the towel tighter around me as he fired up the propellers. When the helicopter lifted off the landing pad a few feet, a gust of wind took it for a little spin. I ducked into the cabin and watched in amazement and horror as he expertly navigated through the turmoil, grateful I wasn't aboard to throw up on his shoes. I heard the yacht's motor starting up, the vibrations traveling up through my feet, setting my teeth chattering, or maybe that was the terror. Then it died just as quickly. Where was everyone? If a crew was piloting the yacht, where were they? Inside the cabin I threw my clothes on, crossed the bar area and made my way to the stairs leading up, presumably to the captain's bridge. When I opened the deck door, I heard the downpour, the harsh rain slapping the wood with loud echoes.

I saw the black sky above me.

"Not good," I muttered, shutting the door. The portholes were blurry with rain. But I needed to find someone from the crew, to tell them I was here and to find out the plan, if there was one. I punched the door open again, and braced against the rain, now streaking sideways and pricking my skin. I was about to head to the bridge, when I heard a voice. I thought it was coming from a speaker on the yacht, but it was actually coming from the deck of a Coast Guard tugboat that had pulled up next to the yacht. From the deck, a tall man in a white T-shirt and jeans yelled my name through a megaphone.

"Cassie! My name is Jake! You must disembark now! We need you off this boat, right away, before this storm gets any worse. Come here and I'll grab your hand. I've been sent to rescue you."

Rescue me? Were it not for the very real weather, causing very real panic, I would have assumed this was, indeed, my rescue fantasy. But there was a storm to survive, and this man's tight expression made it clear to me that this wasn't part of the fantasy at all. I *was* in danger. I clutched a rail, my tunic soaked to my skin. Was it really safer in that tiny little boat than on the enormous solid yacht? Nothing was making sense.

"Cassie! Come closer and grab my hand!"

I stepped out onto the deck and saw the churning sea around me. Wave after wave smashed high over the deck, slapping my legs, sending gallons more water over the polished wood and into the blue pool. Another wave hit, this time sweeping me off my feet and onto my hip with a bang. I sat there, legs splayed, frozen, as I do in times of abject panic. I could no longer hear Jake's voice, just the sound of the angry, black sea. I grabbed onto a lower rail, afraid to stand up. I had the doomed sense that if I let go, I'd be washed over the side of the heaving boat. Before I knew what was happening, an arm like a tree trunk grabbed me around my middle and lifted me off the ground.

"We have to get off this boat, now!" Jake bellowed.

"Okay, then!"

What can I say? I flailed like a scared, wet cat in the driving rain. I clutched where I could, but his T-shirt was slippery and I couldn't get a grip. I went over the side of the boat, felt the sharp sting of the water. For a second I went under and could see only the churning above my head. I screamed underwater, soundlessly, and felt my body buffeted by the swells until at last my head emerged and the scream pierced my own ears. I pulled in a fast breath and had just a second to see that if the boats moved any closer to each other, I would be crushed. Before I could figure out what to do, I saw Jake struggling through the waves to reach me.

"Cassie! Calm down!" Jake yelled, splashing towards me. "You're gonna be okay, but you have to relax."

I tried to listen, tried to remember that I could in fact swim. I helped us move towards the side of the rescue boat and from there he secured my hands around a lower rung on the ladder, climbed ahead a few steps, then reached down and pulled me aboard like I was a wet rag doll. I dropped onto the deck, breathless. He shook out his hair, knocking the sea water from his ears, then took my face in his hands and said, "Good going, Cassie."

"What do you mean?" I asked. "I nearly killed us both! I panicked!"

"But then you calmed down and you helped us swim to the boat. And we're okay now. We're going to be okay." He moved strands of dripping hair away from my face. "Let's get you below deck."

I finally got a good look at the man who had saved me, as he stood up. He was enormous, at least six-foot-five, with a shock of black wavy hair and black eyes. He had the profile of a Greek statue. He caught me looking at his torso and then it struck me. *He knows my name!*

"Are you one of the men from . . ."

"I am," he said, yanking me to my feet. He threw a thick wool blanket around my shoulders and added, "Now that we're here and you're safe, maybe we should get back to the plan. What do you think? Do you accept the Step?"

"I . . . guess so, yes. I do."

"Well, either way, I still have to get us out of here. I am a certified diver and lifeguard, just in case you were wondering."

He placed his firm hands on my trembling shoulders

and ushered me below to a much smaller room, cozier than any I had seen on the yacht, but much less steady. The waves were slapping at the portholes. I made a beeline for a space heater in the corner and used the blanket to cup the warm air on either side of me. I looked around, trying to keep my balance as the storm tossed the boat. The room was dimly lit with gaslight sconces, oak walls and quilted pillows strewn about a high bed. I noticed a quaint kitchenette with an old-fashioned stove and a ceramic sink. It looked like the captain's quarters.

"I'm sorry I panicked. I thought we were moving *away* from the storm. Next thing you know, I was in the storm." I started to sniffle, the events of the last half hour finally catching up to me.

"Shhh . . . it's okay," Jake said. He swiftly crossed the room and took me in his arms. "You're safe now. But I have to leave you here to steer us away from the hurricane."

"Hurricane!"

"Well, initially it was a tropical storm. It turned very quickly. Wait here. And get those wet clothes off. It won't be long until we're safely away," he said, his muscled torso apparent through this wet white T-shirt. This man was romance-cover-model perfect. And though I didn't want to be alone again, he had an authority to his voice that was hard to ignore.

"Get under those covers and warm up. I'll join you soon."

He went to leave, then pivoted and made his way over to where I was standing in front of the heater. When he bent to kiss me, I almost laughed at the image of us, me a naked woman under a blanket being kissed by a giant, shirtless god, one with wet curls and the thickest eyelashes I've ever seen on a man. He placed his lips on mine and pressed, parting them easily, his warm tongue prodding, tentatively at first. He folded over me, his massive hand cradling my head like it was no bigger than a peach. When he pulled away from me it was only reluctantly, I could feel it.

"I won't be long," he said.

"Hurry back." *Hurry back? I might as well have said that in a Southern accent!* We were in real danger and I was swooning like a schoolgirl.

Dropping the damp blanket to the floor, I looked around the room. I opened the small galley closet and found a few blue work shirts hanging there. I peeled off my wet clothes and carefully strung them over a chair in front of the space heater. I threw on one of the flannel shirts. It was so big, *he* was so big, it hung to my knees. I crawled on top of the big bed, feeling the waves. With every passing minute, the Gulf waters seemed calmer and calmer. I thought about the cute pilot and hoped he had reached shore safely. I made a mental note to ask Jake to check for me. There must be some number, some central call-in place where members and participants could reach someone from S.E.C.R.E.T.

The sound of the motor dying down woke me from a nap. I had no idea how long I had been out, but the waves had calmed considerably. I could hear Jake bumping around above me, making his way across the deck to the stairs to the galley, where I lay on the bed waiting. I wasn't good at waiting. Calmness in the face of chaos wasn't my style. But this was, after all, my rescue fantasy. While I decided I didn't like being rescued one bit, I was willing to take part in the aftermath.

"Hi," he said, grinning from ear to ear at the sight of me on the bed.

"Hi."

"Everything's good up there. We're safely away from the storm. Do you mind if I take off the rest of my wet clothes?"

"I don't mind at all," I said, resting back on the pillows. If he was going to rescue me, I was going to play along. "So I'm safe, then?"

"You were never in any danger," he said, shuffling off his damp jeans. This comment pricked the fantasy bubble and left me reeling in reality.

"Are you kidding? I fell off a *boat* into the *Gulf* during a *hurricane!*"

He was so tall he had to duck in the galley as he made his way to the bed.

"Yes, you did, Cassie, but I'm trained to save lives. And yours was never in great danger. I can assure you."

He was so smooth from head to toe that he looked like marble. "But, but what if . . . something had happened to me?"

"It was a tropical storm that became a hurricane very quickly. No one saw it coming, not even the weather bureau."

I had to admit, there is something exciting about surviving an accident. You feel alive in the most visceral way; your veins pulse; you can detect your skin breathing. You feel very fragile and human, but at the same time nearly immortal. Jake tentatively approached the bed. I could smell the salt water on his skin and some other scent beneath that, something velvety and dark.

"Do you still accept the Step?" he asked, his black eyes on me, his hands pushing his wet hair back in a way that reminded me so much of Will.

"I . . . guess," I said, my chin jutting out over my blanket like an impudent child's. "But I don't know if I can feel sexy and terrified at the same time."

"Let me help," he said, taking a fistful of my blanket in one hand.

He drew the blanket away from my shoulders and nestled it around my waist. He took a long look at me, then tugged me closer to him, tilting my head up and putting his salty lips to mine. He loomed over me, making me feel safe again, protected. He told me over and over that I was okay, that I'd be okay, slowly nudging the blanket at my waist to the floor and pushing me back onto the bed. I felt my damp hair spread out around me, and his skin, that expanse of smoothness, meeting every inch of my own flesh. I closed my eyes and let my resolve melt. And I took in his smell: the ocean.

"I'm going to take very good care of you, you know that, right?"

I nodded, too stunned to talk. This was a man the likes of which I'd never seen, never experienced. He made me feel soft and small and delicate. In my constant self-sufficiency, I had forgotten it might be possible to have a man protect me, to be my anchor. I swear to God I trembled as I watched him move to the foot of the bed, gently fold his enormous hands around my ankles, lift a foot to his face, then run his tongue along the tender arch, kissing the tips of my toes, then putting them in his mouth. I couldn't help but giggle. I relaxed back on my elbows as he slipped his hands up the length of my calves, my thighs, and then stopped to look at my face, devouring me with his eyes. He knelt on the bed, resting my legs on either side of him, and parted me. He trailed his hands along my quivering thighs (yes, they really were quivering!). He skimmed over me with his thumbs, not quite touching me there, then up my torso to my breasts. I arched forward, aching for him. I arched in a way that said, *Now, please!* And yet he continued to tease me with his tongue, arousing me so quickly and so fully. *See? See what you're doing to me?* I wanted to say. But I was speechless. Oh God, I had never been with a man this compelling, this strong. He was a work of art.

"Do you want me inside you, Cassie?" he asked, propped up on one elbow, his free hand caressing my breast.

Do I?

"Um . . . yes."

"Say it. Say you want me."

"I . . . want you," I said, with an urgency that had me on the brink of tears.

With that, he trailed a hand from my breasts down to my stomach and thrust his finger inside me. "You *do* want me," he said, a dark smile crossing his lips.

I almost made a joke about going overboard, but I shook it out of my head. His face came towards mine and his kiss was full of vigor and fire. I kissed him back with the same force. It was different from Jesse's kiss, or any kiss I'd ever had. This one was all-consuming. I kissed him like my life depended on it. Then his hand reached beneath a pillow and freed a condom, and he stopped kissing me just long enough to rip the package open with his teeth. He slipped it on with ease and then guided himself into me.

"You'll never be afraid again, Cassie," he said.

I lifted for him, and then with my eyes closed, savored the feel of him. How long had it been since a man entered me? Had I ever been taken so richly, so completely before? Never. My wanting was so intense, it almost felt like my first time.

He was thrusting into me, deeper and deeper, stopping every inch so that I could take him in, breathe into him, and then began to move above me, slowly at first, and then faster, rhythmically, smoothly. I couldn't help but gasp. His arms were beneath me, pulling me towards him so he could move deeper inside me. I couldn't believe how wet I was. My thighs were now wrapped high around his back, the muscles in his arms tensing and twitching.

"Cassie, this is incredible," he said, before nudging me to turn over and slide on top of him, which I did. His hands found my waist and held on, and he lifted me until we found our rhythm again. Then he put his thumb to me, bringing yet another part of me alive.

"I could do this to you forever," he said.

But it was too much to bear. I threw my head back, my hands on his chest. He was so far inside me it felt like he was part of me, and as he stroked in and out, something in me ignited as he touched a spot, the sweetest spot I owned.

Pleasure swam to the surface, moving me out of the way so it could take over. "Baby, you're going to make me come." The words tumbled out of my mouth.

He pushed into me, into that spot inside of me, until I had no choice but to let go. It was like a wave, inside and out. I rode him hard, and as I did I could feel him tense up and let out a low, deep moan. I didn't care anymore about falling, about the danger, about where I was, and what was happening outside with the sea. Only what was happening inside mattered, here on the bed, in this boat, with this Greek god of a man who'd plucked me from the water and who I was now straddling on a high, soft bed.

Moments later I collapsed across his chest. I felt him recede inside of me until he gently eased himself out. And then he lay there, lazily stroking my back, tugging at my damp hair, and muttering, over and over again, "Incredible."

That night, lying in my own bed, my journal in my lap, Dixie on the pillow next to me, I still felt some leftover vertigo from the boat. The Spinster Hotel seemed to be gently rocking from side to side.

I tried to put down in words why this sea adventure had been so transformative. Was it the thrilling ride to the yacht, surviving the plunge over the side of it, or sex in the rescue boat with a man who did everything so beautifully? Was it coming on deck with him to sip hot chocolate and watch the sunset, so vivid after the storm? Was it when he slipped my Step Five charm into my hand, *Fearlessness* engraved on the back? Yes, it was all of those moments and more. I remembered Matilda telling me that fear can't be released without our permission. Since we ourselves generate it, only we can let it go. And that's exactly what I had done. There was fear. I felt it. Then I let it go.

IX

A few weeks after my spill into the Gulf and that incredible session on the tugboat, a newfound fear-lessness manifested in me. I began to stand up to Tracina's subtle bullying at work. I wasn't mean about it, but when she was late, I left my shift on time rather than help-fully waiting until she got there. I decided it was Will's problem to fill the gap, and to scold her, not mine. I also started to wear my hair in a low ponytail, which showed off my new blond highlights. I dipped into the insurance money I had received when Scott died and bought some new clothes, a luxury I'd never allow myself before. I bought a couple pairs of tight black pants, and bright v-neck T-shirts. I finally got up the nerve to duck into Trashy Diva, a retro clothing and lingerie store in the French Quarter that Tracina frequented. I bought some pretty bras and matching thongs and a sexier nightie to sleep in. Nothing too risqué, but it was a step up from my usual cotton fare. I wasn't irresponsible with money. I just wanted my outside to reflect the vividness that I was beginning to feel on the inside. My runs became more regular, too, after work, taking in the three-mile loop around the French Quarter. I saw parts of the city I had always ignored, so stuck had I been in my own routine. I even volunteered the Café to staff the booth for the New Orleans Revitalization Society's fund-raiser costume ball, though Will balked at first. "Don't we have enough to do with the Café renovations?"

It was true that the Café was going through a very slow renaissance, one that was consuming much of Will's free time, to Tracina's chagrin. He had started with painting the interior and buying new stainless steel appliances. His big plan was to open up the second floor for fine dining and music, but after installing a small washroom near the land-ing, city hall stalled the permits. He threw a mattress on the floor and if he wasn't sleeping at Tracina's, that's where I'd sometimes find him, planning, ruminating or just pouting. For now, he had to content himself with hauling old junk from upstairs, stuff that had been up there since the place was a PJ's Coffee franchise, to the dump.

"Altruism is good advertising, Will," I said. "Giving is good for the soul." I flashed back to the scene in the Mansion's kitchen months ago, when I'd learned the inher-ent benefits of giving. So much change in so little time.

In volunteering for the booth, for the first time in my life I actually threw myself into one of New Orleans's unique popular pastimes: joining things. I had never before been a joiner of clubs, or groups, or charities, or anything for that matter. And while reading the society pages never made me long for money or prestige, it did give me the sense that there was a whole other world out there, one where community mattered and where camaraderie could be fun. I had lived in the city for almost six years. One of the Café regulars once told me that New Orleans "claims you at seven." I was starting to understand what he meant. This place was finally feeling like home. I told Matilda as much when I saw her for one of our post-Step discussions at Tracey's.

"It takes seven years to make a home," she said. She was a transplant herself decades ago, albeit one from the South. She also offered the deepest apologies for the spill over the yacht and the terror it caused. "That was not part of the scenario. We were going to fake the engine dying where Jake could find you, never dreaming it actually *would* die. Let alone during a tropical storm!"

"Tropical storm? It was a hurricane, Matilda," I said, eyebrows up.

"Right. I'm sorry. But you certainly earned that Step Five charm," she said, pointing to my beautifully cluttered bracelet. I held the pale gold up to the light and watched the charms shimmer. While I loved collecting them, I was craving constancy in my life. I had begun to imagine what it would be like to have one man in my life, one devoted only to me. As much as the fantasies were changing my life and the way I felt about myself, I did feel a void. I didn't want to mention that to Matilda. I had four fantasies left, and I knew she'd urge me to see these through and not rush into a relationship before I was ready, if at all. But soon I'd be finished with S.E.C.R.E.T. Then what? Will I want to become part of S.E.C.R.E.T. or will I want to take my experiences and find someone special to build a life with? Was I ready? And who would want me? I had so many questions for Matilda.

"You're on an exploration," she said over drinks at Tracey's. "Who you are as a person, your likes and dislikes, they come first. Then your partner's. Do you understand?"

"But what if I tell the next man I'm serious about that I was a member of S.E.C.R.E.T., and it freaks him out?"

"Then he's not the man for you," she said, shrugging. "Any man who'd balk at a single, healthy woman being intimate with other consenting adults, *joyfully and safely* intimate, isn't worth your time, Cassie. Besides, you don't owe a new lover a full inventory of your past sexual behavior, especially if it doesn't affect him in the least. Especially if it *benefits* him!"

I looked at my bracelet again. I didn't wear it every day, but when I did have it on, I felt infused with something special. Maybe it had to do with the words embossed on the charms: *Surrender, Courage, Trust, Generosity,* and now *Fearlessness.* So far, beyond the comment from Will at the auction, no one at the Café had mentioned it. Not even Tracina, who was like a magpie when she saw shiny things.

"These words really mean something to me," I said to Matilda. I was surprised I had said this out loud.

"Well, that is the paradox, Cassie, one I hope you're learning to embrace. In some ways a moment of bliss doesn't mean anything. But if you can learn to let it happen and then let it go, it can begin to mean everything."

I'd known men who couldn't imagine being with only one woman, who'd die for the chance to experience all their sexual fantasies, no strings attached, with several dream women recruited specifically to do their bidding. It wasn't that I was ungrateful to Matilda and to S.E.C.R.E.T., but the urge to bond, to draw one special someone nearer to me, was becoming harder to resist. Why had I rejected Will years ago? I had always found him attractive. Incredibly so. But back then, I felt that if he got closer to me, he'd see me for what I was—boring, afraid, unlovable. Now, for the first time I was beginning to believe I was none of those things. I was gathering a sense of self, a belief that I might be worthy of a man like Will. Sadly, it was happening just as he was developing a deeper relationship with Tracina.

I still looked forward to seeing Will at work. I perked up when I heard his truck pull in, felt jittery when we were alone, the two of us, in the office. And with plans for Café Rose to man the donation booth at the New Orleans Revitalization Society Ball, we were spending more time than ever together designing the banners for the booth. More time than he was spending with Tracina.

The night before the ball, Tracina recruited me to help her help Will with his costume. She couldn't sew, but she certainly knew how to boss me around while I did. The theme of this year's ball was "Make-Believe"; guests would dress as their favorite fictional or fairy-tale characters. After the dinner, the city's most eligible bachelors and bachelorettes would be auctioned off to top bidders, winners getting a dance with their prizes. Tracina had signed up both Will and herself for the auction. She may have lacked social standing, but Tracina was a stunner and would likely go for a good price. And Will, despite being the proprietor of a rather diminutive café, did come from one of the oldest families in the State of Louisiana. Still, he was a reluctant participant.

"Come on, Will! It'll be fun," Tracina said. "And it's for charity."

I was holding a mouthful of pins, working on the hem of his pants. Will was going as Huck Finn, with short pants, suspenders, straw hat and a fishing pole. Tracina was going as Tinker Bell, white tutu, wings and a wand. Dressing like an irritating pixie seemed a perfect choice for her, I thought, as I watched her prance around the kitchen. She was holding the wand, touching everyone on the head.

"Dell, I hereby grant you one wish," she said, touching her head with the wand.

"If you poke me with that thing again, I will snap it in half and shove it up your ass."

Tracina made a *nyah-nyah* face at Dell, then pointed her wand at me like an imaginary pistol.

"Bang! Listen, I can't work that booth with you, Cassie. I'm dancing! And you better dance too."

"I'm not going to have fun. I'm going to help."

"Come on, it's a ball. When do you ever go out? Anyway, what are you dressing up as?"

"Nothing," I said. "My shift ends when dinner's served. And if you're not taking over in the booth, I'll have to find someone who will."

"I'll help," Will offered.

"But you're my date," Tracina whined. "We'll get Dell to do it. But you have to wear a costume, Cassie, and I know the perfect one. Cinderella!"

The thought of me in a ball gown was laughable, and when I said as much, Tracina laughed too.

"No, I meant Cinderella *before* the ball! When she was a scullery maid doing all the sewing and cleaning while her evil stepsisters had a great time. It's perfect for you!"

I wasn't sure if Tracina was being insulting or funny. Will was standing shirtless above me, his baggy pants held up with one hand, looking a little too much like a statue of David. He wasn't a gym rat, but he had an impressively flat stomach and muscled arms. I tried hard not to stare.

"Cassie, why are you being 'Miss I'm Not Participating'?" he asked. "That's not very local of you."

"I guess I'm still working on my citizenship."

Tracina warned Will that she wanted to score a dance with the guest of honor, Pierre Castille, the billionaire who owned acres of waterfront property along Lake Pontchartrain, which had been in his family for generations. He was a private man who had a reputation for ducking in and out the back door at every function.

Kay Ladoucer, a local doyenne and the most conservative member of the city council, was the chair of the ball going on four years. She had arranged for Pierre to make an appearance during this year's ball. Will was not a big fan of Kay. He had had a run-in with her during his bid to expand the restaurant upstairs. Kay argued that until he updated the electrical in the whole building, he couldn't expand. But Will couldn't afford to do that unless he was allowed to expand. So there was a stalemate over the proper permits, despite the fact that half the places on Frenchmen Street had ancient wiring.

If Tracina's tactic bothered Will, he tried hard not to show it. Besides, Pierre Castille's attendance was never a sure thing. At one of the organizational meetings, I overheard Kay complain that he wouldn't give an exact time of arrival, nor would he allow promoters to mention he was coming, nor would he participate in the auction or even commit to attending the meal.

Will glanced down at me looking about as miserable as I'd ever seen him. I gave him a sympathetic shrug and hoisted the hem another inch higher, reminding myself that Will was another woman's man, regardless of whether Tracina was as engaged with him as he was with her, something I was beginning to question. For the past few weeks, she'd disappear and be unreachable for hours, and I knew Will well enough to sense his jealous funk.

"She probably had an appointment for her brother," he'd say, craning his neck, watching the parking spots in front of the Café, waiting for her to pull up. "Or maybe she's shopping. She's always running off to shop."

I'd smile and nod, careful not to contradict him, finding it fascinating the way we lie to ourselves when we don't want something to be true. I'd done it for years with Scott. But one of the many gifts of S.E.C.R.E.T. was that my experiences were teaching me to stop lying to myself. In the middle of the kitchen while I was hemming Will's pants, his eyes met mine for a little longer than usual. I told myself it meant nothing. When he offered to drive me home later, I reminded myself that my place was on his way home.

But when he idled the truck while waiting for me to get safely inside the Spinster Hotel and playfully blew me a kiss from the cab, I wondered if I was lying to myself all over again.

The New Orleans Revitalization Society was one of the oldest of its kind in the city, dating back to post–Civil War days. Back then it used to raise money to build schools in the neighborhoods where freed slaves began to settle. After the devastation of Hurricane Katrina, the Society made rebuilding schools in disadvantaged wards its focus, because waiting for the government to do it meant waiting forever. My volunteering for the Society was part of my attempt to make this city my home, and to make friends beyond the Café and its environs. My job for the evening was to work the donation booth, to collect checks and run through credit cards. No costume and dancing for me. I wanted to take this event seriously. In exchange for my time, Kay allowed us to hang a Café Rose banner on the skirt of the table.

This year the ball was being held at the New Orleans Museum of Art, one of my favorite buildings in the city. I loved its four-columned Greek Revival facade, and its square marble foyer surrounded on all sides by a high balcony. I used to wander in its echoing rooms when I was still married to Scott and things were tense between us. I would visit Degas' *Girl in Green* painting, because she seemed mournful to me, facing away, either worried about the past or afraid of the future. Or maybe I was just projecting. I had an hour to assemble the booth and to get a rundown from Kay. I found her, dressed like the Red Queen from Alice in Wonderland, yelling in the middle of the white marble foyer.

"Move the ladder!"

Two young men were trying to suspend giant sparkly snowflakes from the ceiling. Kay wasn't a big fan.

"I don't know how snowflakes fit the 'Make-Believe' theme, but what else can we suspend from the ceiling? Fairies?"

An image of Tracina dangling from a thread brought a smile to my face, interrupted only by Kay eyeing me over her reading glasses.

"Where are you setting up the booth? Not in here, I hope!"

"I think over there," I said, pointing to an area near the back of the room.

"*No!* I don't want people to confuse our beautiful dinner with a grubby cash grab! Near the coat check, please. And where are your tools?"

"Tools? I didn't realize that—"

Kay let out an exasperated huff. "I'll get a couple of the maintenance guys to help."

By the time Tracina arrived, fully decked out in her white tutu and tiara, the booth was up and running and I was comfortably hidden behind its high skirt.

"Where's Will?" I asked, as casually as possible.

"Parking the truck. I'm going to get a drink. You want one?"

"I'm good, thanks."

The first of the guests started to arrive. I spotted a Snow White, several Scarletts, a Rhett Butler, two Draculas, an Ali Baba and a Harry Potter. There was a Dorothy, a Mad Hatter, a Black Beard the pirate and a Blue Beard, the murderous aristocrat. I glanced down at my A-line skirt and plain blouse. Maybe I should have put more effort into the occasion. Did I really need to wear a waitressing apron? Well, there was the matter of storing pens and credit card slips. And I wasn't there to meet men. I was there to work for a charity. But just as I was securing the second Café Rose banner to the back of the booth, I heard, "Cassie, over here!" A beautiful woman in a Scheherazade costume waved at me from the crowd forming near the booth. It was Amani, the tiny Indian doctor who sat next to me my first day at S.E.C.R.E.T. headquarters. She looked magnificent in layered red and pink scarves enhancing a nearly sixty-year-old body, one that still had formidable curves and definite presence. It was her eyes, though, that stood out above all else—sparkling with mischief, black-lined, framed by a vivid red veil.

"What are you doing here?" I asked. It was odd to see a S.E.C.R.E.T. member out in the community.

"Believe it or not, *our* little group gives very generously to this cause every year, but not under our name. Here," she said, thrusting an envelope at me. I thanked her for the donation. "Matilda's on her way too. You won't miss her. She's dressed as a fairy godmother. Naturally."

Before I could say anything, Kay was by my side, watching as guest after guest slipped envelopes into the box on the table.

"Dr. Lakshmi," Kay said, offering a hand. "You look absolutely stunning."

"Thank you, Kay," Amani said with a slight bow. "See you soon, Cassie, I hope."

Kay didn't ask how I had managed to be on a first-name basis with an esteemed member of the community.

"The auction hasn't begun yet and it sure looks like we're going to reach our quota!" she said.

"Here's hoping."

Dinner was a six-course extravaganza of local specialties: lobster étouffée and grits with truffles and brandy. Filet mignon with crab béarnaise. Dessert was a rich bread pudding topped with crème fraîche and gold flakes. Once the plates were cleared, it was my cue to leave. But I was curious about the auction, curious to see who would win Will.

"Okay, it's time to start the bidding!" Kay said, hurrying to the front of the room. "We can't keep waiting for *him*." She meant Pierre Castille. Tracina wasn't the only woman hoping to spend some time with him.

I watched as the female bidders gathered closer to the stage where Kay had gathered the men for auction. Besides Will, the bachelor auction included our very young state senator, whom I would have cultivated a crush on had he been a Democrat. There was an aging but still handsome municipal judge who had taken up marathon running after his wife died, earning the sympathy and the eye of every single *single* woman over fifty. And an attractive African-American actor from a TV show that was shot in New Orleans. You'd have thought the hot actor would garner the highest bid, but in fact, the esteemed judge went for $12,500 to the president of the Garden District Historical Society. The actor scored a distant second, bringing in $8,000.

Watching all the raucous fun and the bawdy energy of the auction from behind the booth, I started to feel like a wall-flower again. Why did I always observe life in action instead of being a full participant? When was I going to learn?

"And our final bachelor," Kay announced, "is Will Foret, the second-generation owner of the esteemed Café Rose, one of the finest on Frenchmen. He's thirty-seven years old, ladies, and he's single. Who will start the bidding?"

Will looked mortified, but still sexy in his Huck Finn costume, with the fishing pole and the baggy pants held up by suspenders. The room seemed to agree. When the bidding heated up, Tracina began to panic. When the tally reached $15,000, Tracina grabbed the mike from Kay's hand.

"This man isn't actually single," she said. "We've been dating for more than three years and we're thinking of moving in together." She'd been drinking too much champagne, and if I thought that Will couldn't be more embarrassed, I was wrong. He now turned dark crimson.

Finally, an elderly woman in a tarnished tiara made the winning offer of $22,000, to which Kay issued a resounding, "Sold!" Will, the highest priced bachelor of the night, was escorted to his awaiting purchaser.

"That ends the men's auction," Kay said with a smack of her gavel. "But please refresh your drinks. The ladies' auction is next and we need another $75,000 dollars, friends. So don't put your checkbooks away!"

Just then, a hush fell over the room. Two security guards entered the ballroom, parting a sea of people. They were followed by a tall man wearing a smart tuxedo, black bow tie, black shirt and aviator glasses tinted light blue. He had a motorcycle helmet under his arm, which he quickly handed off to a security guard standing next to him. He removed his sunglasses and folded them into his pocket.

"I'm sorry I'm late," he announced. "I couldn't find anything to wear."

It was Pierre Castille, his sandy hair slightly tousled by the helmet. He casually greeted the handful of people who'd gathered to say hello, including a clearly flustered Kay, who left the microphone to race across the floor meet him. His easy grin made him look less like a reclusive scion than a stylish indie rocker. When he turned away from Kay and made for my booth, my heart raced. I cursed Tracina for abandoning me. I looked down and busied myself with credit card slips, trying not to appear starstruck.

"Is this where I can leave my donation?"

When I glanced up, he was leaning on the booth with one hand. He didn't look entirely uncomfortable in a tuxedo, which was refreshing. For a second I forgot how to speak.

"I—yes, you can place a check in the box if you like, or I can take a credit card."

"Wonderful," he said, holding eye contact with me for what felt like forever. My God he was sexy. "What's your name?"

I actually looked over my shoulder to make sure he was talking to me. The whole room was watching, including Will, who moved through the crowd towards us.

"Cassie. Cassie Robichaud."

"Robichaux? Of the Mandeville Robichauxs?"

By then I was shocked to see Will at the booth, offering his hand to Pierre.

"She spells it with a Northern D, not a Southern X," he said.

"Well, if it isn't Will Foret the Second. What's it been? Fifteen years?"

I watched in amazement as *my* Will shook hands with *the* Pierre Castille, Tracina pushing through the crowd to reach them.

"About that long, yeah."

"Good to see you, Will," he said. "Too bad our fathers aren't around. They'd have been happy to see this."

"Yours, maybe," Will said, tipping his Huck hat. "Cassie, I'll see you at work tomorrow."

I watched him walk right past Tracina and out the door.

"So, Cassie Robichaud, not from Mandeville. Where were we?"

"Funnily enough I live on Mandeville Street in Marigny, but I'm from Michigan. But it's a French name from my dad's side. But I'm not sure really about its origins . . ." *You're talking too much, Cassie!*

"Right. I'll be sure to stop by the booth to make a donation before I leave," he said, bowing slightly.

Rich, powerful people didn't easily dazzle me, but this man had charisma.

Suddenly, Tracina was eager to volunteer. "I'll take over from here," she said, ducking behind the booth. "Will left, so I can stay and help. You can go home now. Besides, you don't have a costume."

"Did you know Will knew him?" I asked.

"They're childhood friends."

"I see. Okay, then. Um, I guess it's time for me to leave."

"Yes, run really fast," she said, not looking at me, watching Pierre take a seat near the front of the room.

The bachelorette auction would soon be under way. I looked down at my outfit. Tracina had been right all along. I was just the scullery maid. Now that the dishes were done, it was time to go. I made my way through the lobby, looking for Will. Instead I spotted Matilda talking on a cell phone, heading straight for me. She said goodbye to whomever she was speaking with and snapped the phone shut. That's when I noticed her costume, a stunning mermaid dress covered in emerald sequins, a small crown perched on her head.

"Cassie! Wait! Where are you going?"

"I finished my shift at the donation booth. I'm going home. Thanks by the way for the donation. It was very gen—"

"No, you're not going home," she said, grabbing me by the arm, turning me around and trotting me towards a door marked PRIVATE. "I realize we've kept this well under wraps, but tonight is . . . well, it's your special night, Cassie."

"Tonight?" I said, realizing with a shock that she meant she had a fantasy in store for me. "But I'm wearing—"

"Don't worry. Help is on the way."

She waved a card at a small white security box on the wall and a door clicked open. Inside was a cozy dressing room where Amani and another woman I vaguely recognized were perched on silk-covered stools. They stood when we entered, agitation on their faces. To their left was a dressing table with a mirror framed by lightbulbs, makeup carefully organized on a white towel. Hanging on a rack nearby was a beautiful pale pink dress that hung to the floor. I wasn't really a girly-girl, but this satiny ball gown tickled something very ancient in my DNA. Beneath it was a pair of stunning sparkly pumps.

Matilda cleared her throat.

"We'll explain later, Cassie, but for now, we have to get you ready. Fast. It's about to begin."

"What's about to begin?"

"Never mind," she said.

This was all meant for me? The dress, the makeup. I was going to be on display, but for whom, and to what end?

"You remember Michelle? From S.E.C.R.E.T. headquarters? She's your stylist." I did remember her round angelic face and easy giggle. Stylist? What were they getting me styled for?

"Cassie, I'm so excited for you, but we have to hurry. Undergarments first. Off with them."

Before I had a chance to react, Michelle shoved me behind a bamboo dressing screen, and tossed a gossamer silk bra, thong and pale stay-up stockings over the top.

"I bet you thought birds and butterflies would be helping you," she said, laughing. I had no idea what she meant.

Once I had the garments on, Michelle gave me a bathrobe, then seated me in front of the mirror. She gathered my long hair into a low chignon at the nape of my neck. Amani painted my cheeks and lips light pink, then gave the rest of my face a natural glow with a big brush. After adding a hint of mascara, we were done.

"Time for the dress," Michelle said, carefully plucking the pink confection off the hanger and ushering me behind the screen again.

All the while, Matilda kept coming and going from the room.

"How much longer?" she asked Amani.

How much longer for what? I lifted the heavy dress over my shoulders and felt it slide easily down my body and fall perfectly around my hips. I stepped out to get help with the zipper, and when I caught a glimpse of myself in the mirror, I was rendered speechless. The dress was beautiful, a pale pink like the lining of a seashell. It cinched me so snugly at the waist, I realized I actually had one. The sheen was the barest sateen, and the dress was strapless and cut sweet-heart-style across my chest, showing off my shoulders and arms. The skirt flared out like a ballerina's, with a soft crinoline underneath to keep its shape.

"You look . . . beautiful," said Matilda.

"But how is this going to play out? People know me. My boss's girlfriend is still here. The whole city's here!"

"Trust us, Cassie. It'll all be fine," Matilda said, glancing at her watch.

Admittedly, some of the other fantasies had taken me by surprise, especially Jesse, but this was different. This was the first time I was around people I knew, in my real life. It was exciting and dangerous, but it also filled me with anxiety. Michelle gently removed a tiara, a delicate twist of silver and sparkle, from a small velvet bag. She nested it across the top of my head, framing my tousled chignon.

Matilda and I looked at each other in the mirror.

"Stunning, my dear. But don't forget these," she said, handing me the sparkly white pumps.

I slid my feet into them and took a few practice steps in my heels, feeling utterly ridiculous and overjoyed at the same time. Yes, I could dance in these; in fact, I suspected I would be doing just that after the auction, which by my estimation should be over by now. I was glad to have missed that part.

"It's time!" Matilda announced, taking me by the arm and tugging me across the foyer towards the ballroom.

"What? Where are we going? The dance hasn't started," I protested.

But Matilda wasn't listening. We were moving so quickly, I had to place a hand on my tiara to keep it from falling off. We reached the ballroom and I entered behind Matilda, making sure she was screening me from view. As I peeked around her shoulder, I saw a line of beautiful women, each taking a seat onstage. Among them was an attractive local news anchor, a model who looked like a young Naomi Campbell, an actress from the same TV show as one of the men who had been auctioned, a pretty blond cellist from the New Orleans symphony, two beautiful Italian sisters who owned one of the top spas in town, a few "daughters of" . . . and Tracina, who was now more than a little tipsy in her slightly off-kilter tutu.

"There's one more empty stool," Kay announced into the microphone, cupping her hand over her eyebrows to scan the back of the room. "But maybe she left."

Please make me invisible, I prayed. *I can't cross the room in this dress, to be auctioned off in that crowd. I'd make a fool out of myself.*

"She hasn't left!" Matilda yelled, pushing me forward.

"There she is!" Kay crooned. "It's Miss Cassie Robichaud, one of our lovely volunteers. Now, doesn't she look enchanting!"

Matilda placed her hands on my shrunken shoulders. She must have been able to tell I had died a little inside. She whispered in my ear, "Remember, Cassie, this is Step Six: *Confidence*. You have it in you already. Find it. Now."

With one last nudge, I was launched into the crowd, and I made my way slowly, eyes heavy on me. I curved around the tables, my skirt brushing chair legs and calves. As I crossed the empty dance floor and headed to the stage, the dress elicited some *oohs* and *aahs*. But the healthy wolf whistle from the balcony actually made me laugh a little. Had it really been meant for me? When I passed Pierre's table, I tried to avoid eye contact with him. I climbed the stairs and passed Tracina, perched on her stool like an agitated bird.

"You seem more and more interesting the longer I know you," she hissed as I took my seat.

"Let's begin, shall we?" Kay started the bidding with the news anchor, who, after a fierce back and forth, went for $7,500 to the general manager of one of the waterfront casinos. The model, who'd made aggressive attempts to get Pierre's attention, was crestfallen when Mark "Sharky" Allen, the Gem and Jewel King with the cheesy late-night commercials, battled it out to the tune of $16,000 to win a dance with her. The sisters went as a package deal and two of the debutantes attracted five-figure bids. Tracina kept primping and preening while she eyed Pierre at his table close to the stage. But it was Carruthers Johnstone, the exceptionally tall, broad-shouldered district attorney from Orleans Parish, who opened and closed bidding on Tracina for $15,000, a hell of a sum that caused the room to erupt in a round of applause.

I was never going to garner that kind of money. Tracina had those long legs and a vivacious personality. She was funny and hip. She could work a room. She could stand up for herself. Even dressed as a pixie she was sexy as all get out. I felt even more humiliated as the event came close to an unceremonious end.

"We are still short of our goal, but we do have one more bachelorette up for auction. Cassie works as a waitress at Café Rose, one of our esteemed sponsors. So I guess, let's open bidding at $500, shall we?"

Oh God, oh God, someone take pity on me and get this over with. I'll actually pay you back if you just give me one low bid and get me off this podium, I thought. But when a man's voice said, "I'll start the bidding at $5,000," I was sure I had misheard. The spotlight was on me and I could hardly see the faces in the crowd.

"Did you say $500, Mr. Castille?" Kay asked.

Mr. Castille? Did Pierre Castille just bid $500? For me?

"No. I said $5,000, Kay. I'd like to open the bidding at $5,000," he said, stepping towards the podium and into the spotlight where I could finally see him. His eyes looked me over like I was a sweet confection he'd never tried before. I clasped my hands in my lap, then crossed my legs, then uncrossed them.

"That's . . . that's very generous, Monsieur Castille. We open at $5,000. Anyone willing to go higher?"

"$6,000," said a voice in the back, a voice belonging to . . . Will.

He came back? Tracina shifted on her stool and pursed her glossy lips. What was Will thinking? He didn't have that kind of money!

"$7,000," said Pierre, glancing over at Will. I felt sick to my stomach, then felt amazing. Then sick again.

"$8,000," Will choked.

Tracina shot me an angry look and threw the same one at Will, who was moving to the front of the room to stand beside Pierre. What was Will *doing*? Kay was about to slap the gavel down to announce a victory to Will, when Pierre announced, "I bid $50,000." The crowd gasped in astonishment. "Does that get you to your goal, Kay?"

Kay was dumbfounded. "Monsieur Castille, $50,000 gets us well *past* that. Any other takers?"

The look on Will's face almost made me cry. He dropped his head and smiled the smile of the defeated.

"And, sold!" Kay yelled, closing the bidding with a pound of her gavel against the podium. Let the dancing begin!"

The crowd immediately began to chatter and rise from their seats, making their way to the empty space in front of the stage.

Tracina sprung off her stool and disappeared among the throng to find her bidder. Pierre stood at the edge of the stage, a grin on his face, Will standing awkwardly beside him.

"Good try, old friend," Pierre said, clapping Will a little too hard on the back. "I'll be sure to stop by the Café now that I have a good reason to."

"You do that," he said. "Cassie, I hope you don't . . . Oh forget it. I'm going home."

Before I could say anything, Will disappeared in the crowd.

"You look magnificent, Miss Robichaud," Pierre said. "Fit for a prince," he added as he took my hand and led me to the center of the dance floor, his bodyguards never far behind.

I could sense the question in everyone's minds as they watched us: *Who is this girl who has so captivated Pierre Castille?* And even though other couples were now joining the dance floor, it felt like Pierre and I were the only two people in the room. He pulled me so close I could feel his breath on my neck. When the band started and he began to move me around the floor, I thought I would faint.

"Why me?" I asked. "You can have any girl you want."

"Why you? You'll understand why after you accept the Step," he said, holding me even tighter.

Pierre Castille is a S.E.C.R.E.T. participant? "I . . . but . . . you?"

"Cassie, do you accept?"

It took me a few seconds to absorb the fact that this man was a participant. Who else in this room was part of S.E.C.R.E.T., or knew about it? Kay? The D.A.? A debutante or two? The room spun along with my mind until the band ended the song with a flourish. Pierre released me and kissed my hand.

"Thank you for the dance, Miss Cassie Robichaud. Until we meet again."

I wanted to scream, *Wait! I do accept the Step!* But did I? What about Will? Pierre bowed deeply, then left the room surrounded by his security guards, stranding me alone on the dance floor. I looked around for Matilda, Amani, anyone besides Tracina, but of course Tracina was the first to get to me.

"Aren't you a little mystery," she said, fist on the waistband of her wilted tutu.

"Where's Will?" I asked, craning my neck to try to find him.

"Gone."

Before I could say anything else, a security guard grabbed my elbow. "Miss Robichaud, there's an urgent call for you. Please come with me," he said, to my and Tracina's astonishment.

The guard guided me out of the ballroom, across the marble lobby and into a waiting limo, eyes on me the whole time. My head was spinning. What a night. The entire community had seen me being picked, chosen, desired. It was all so heady and so lovely. But to enjoy it fully, I had to push thoughts of Will out of my head.

In the limo, I found a chilled glass of champagne in the armrest. I took a sip and sank back into the leather seat as the driver took us down a private ramp where a cluster of security guards appeared. Before I could even blink, Pierre pushed through them, secretly ducking into the limo with me. It was all so swiftly executed, it seemed second nature to everyone except me.

"We'll exit from the back, out the parking garage," he instructed.

The driver nodded and then closed the window between the front and back of the limo.

"Hello," Pierre said, facing me now, grinning and a little flushed. "That went well, I think."

"I . . . yes, it did," I stammered, while playing with the folds of my dress. It truly was the prettiest piece of clothing I'd ever worn, let alone seen.

"So. Do you accept the Step?"

I was still wrapping my mind around the fact that the Bayou Billionaire was a participant in S.E.C.R.E.T. I flashed back to the opening night of Halo, the time I saw him chatting with Kay Ladoucer in the lobby. I reddened slightly, remembering that distinguished British man and the things he did with his hands. Was Pierre participating in a fantasy that night too?

"Cassie, the rules say this is the last time I get to ask: do you accept the Step?"

I waited a beat, then nodded.

His kiss came at me so quickly, it took me several seconds to catch up. When I did, I had no problem matching his ardor. He pulled me on top of him, kissing my clavicle, my shoulders, my neck, his arms completely wrapped around me. Then through the limo window, I caught the briefest glimpse of Tracina holding hands with the D.A. What? No!

"Is that Carruthers Johnstone?" I asked Pierre, breathless.

S . E . C . R . E . T .

Pierre turned just as the giant man scooped Tracina up and placed her on the trunk of a car, kissing her deeply.

"Yes. Bit of a ladies' man, I'm afraid."

"Oh, poor Will," I muttered.

"Cassie." Pierre cupped my chin, making me stare directly into the greenest, most mischievous eyes I'd ever seen. "I'm right here. We have to get you out of this dress. Right now."

I couldn't, wouldn't think about Will right now. Not while I was in the back of a limo with one of the sexiest men in the city.

"What about the driver?"

"One-way glass. We can see him, but he can't see us. No one can."

With that, he reached around me and I felt the delicate zipper of my dress snake down my back, the bodice peeling away from me, leaving me surrounded by pink crinoline and sateen, a cupcake melting in his lap. He began to sort through the folds, grabbing a lush handful of fabric and lifting the whole garment over my head. My tiara caught in the folds, ripping my chignon loose, so by the time he got the dress fully off and tossed it to the other side of the limo, I was a flushed mess, wearing only a lacy strapless bra, a silk thong and my sparkling heels, my hair cascading down around my bare shoulders.

"Unbelievable," he said, pressing me back into the seat opposite him. "I want to see all of you. Take the rest off, Cassie."

I was emboldened by the auction, the dance, the champagne, the privacy of this fast-moving limo, and his obvious attraction, and so I did. I slowly unfastened my bra and let it drop to the floor. Then, I hooked one finger under the band of my thong and eased it down to my ankles, and flicked it off with a toss of my foot. Then I pushed back into the plush seat and opened my legs to him, heels still on. What had become of the shy Cassie who couldn't leave her bedroom wearing a bathrobe? I was jelly in that seat, my legs weakened and shaking. Our eyes looked so deeply into each other that I didn't think it would be possible to break the gaze.

"Amazing," he said, waiting a beat before springing forward to bury his face in my breasts, his hand isolating a nipple and sucking and licking it, slowly then urgently. It was, *he* was, so sexy. He slowly slid a finger inside me. My hands drove through his soft hair, his kisses trailing back and forth between my breasts, until his mouth moved down over my fluttering belly. My God, this was all too much! I was quaking with every kiss.

"I'm going to make you scream, Cassie," he said, before dipping down into me, his tongue landing on that exquisite spot.

"Oh God." It was all I could say as I fell back on my elbows and gave myself up to the sensations. He kissed down my thighs, teasing me, then his warm mouth closed down around me, pulling me fast into that magic place. I couldn't stop the pounding waves of pleasure, nor did I want to. I fully submitted, my legs splayed, my body melting into the seat.

And then I passed that point, that white-hot turning point that his mouth brought me to so easily. I could hear his voice, the catch of his breath. I let the sweet tornado build inside me, knowing he was just beginning.

As I lay there panting, he ripped his clothes off as though they were burning his skin. He sheathed himself with a free hand, while I reached out and grabbed for the muscle of his arms, holding on as he entered me.

"You feel so good," he said hoarsely.

The determination on his face was so sexy. I had to touch it, and when I did, his mouth captured my fingers and sucked them as he rocked inside me, a whole new level of desire filling me. My legs wrapped around his slim hips and I moved with him, gripping his buttocks, careful not to dig too hard with my nails but loving the feel of his firm flesh in my hands. He never lost tempo with my body, even when the car turned. He said my name over and over again, until at last I felt him shudder and stiffen, his arm scooped beneath me, arching me into that sweet space I was coming to know so well. And then he brought me to a whole new place of bliss. I came again, my body pushing into his as I clutched him between my thighs. I could feel him release, too, and then, slowly, he lowered himself on top of me, holding one of my hands, our fingers entwined, mouths a few inches apart, though we couldn't kiss each other anymore. We had to catch our breath. He pushed away gently, collapsing back on the seat opposite me as I lay gasping.

"I'm sorry if the limo felt a little rushed, but I wanted to rip your dress off when you were on the stage tonight. So I think I exercised some restraint, don't you?"

"Glad you held back." Feeling bold, I asked a few questions of my own. "Have you done this before? With S.E.C.R.E.T.? I mean, you're kind of, um, an eligible guy. Why would you need to do something like this to have *your* sexual fantasies realized?"

"You'd be surprised, Cassie. Anyhow, I'm told I'm not supposed to say too much. Matilda warned me that you were the curious type. I could ask you the same question. Why would such an alluring woman like you need S.E.C.R.E.T.?"

"You'd also be surprised," I said, sitting and gathering up my dress. I felt vulnerable and a little angry that Matilda had told him anything about me.

"Has it been everything you thought it would be?" he asked.

"S.E.C.R.E.T. has taught me a lot," I said, securing the bodice, adjusting the back myself.

"Like what?"

"Like that it might be impossible for one man to fulfill *all* of a woman's desires." Why was I being so insouciant?

"You might be wrong about that," Pierre said, sliding into his boxers and then his tuxedo pants.

"Oh?"

He reached across the seat, put his hand around my wrist and tugged me towards him, until I was kneeling in front of him. His eyes held mine for a few moments before he plunged his face into my neck and buried a firm kiss in the place where it curved into my shoulder. Just then the limo pulled up in front of the Spinster Hotel. He reached into the pocket of his tuxedo jacket and took out a gold charm. My gold charm.

"Ah, let me see. A Roman numeral six, with the word *Confidence* on the back. Very . . . *charming*."

While he grinned at his play on words, I reached for the charm, but Pierre dangled it farther away from me.

"Not so fast," he said, the light in his green eyes now ablaze. "I want you to know something, Cassie. When you're done with this . . . thing you're doing, I'm going to come and find you. And when I do, I'm going to show you that one man *can* fulfill all your desires."

I didn't know whether to feel overjoyed or overwhelmed, but I carried his good-night kiss, and my shoes, up the stairs and past Anna's door on the second floor, where I noticed that her light was still on.

For days after the Ball, my mood careened from ecstatic to morose. I'd flash back to scenes with Pierre in the limousine, and I'd have to squeeze my legs together to contain my longing. Other times, I'd plummet, because the flip side of a fantasy is that despite how real it feels, and how fantastically it's executed, it is not, in fact, real.

Still, it was hard to resist poring over the society pages in the *Times-Picayune*, one of those New Orleans mainstays in a city that loved its benefits and balls. There I was, photographed in the background, of course, because Pierre Castille was the focus of the evening. The caption described me as the "Cinderella Seductress" who "captivated the Bayou Bachelor." This provided endless fodder even for Dell, who seemed more impatient with me than she was with Tracina.

"Hey, Cinderella Seductress," Dell teased, "any chance you could look after table ten for me? I got a prince picking me up tonight in a giant pumpkin. Pulling up right here on Frenchmen Street. Got any shoes I can borrow?"

Tracina, on the other hand, had grown more subdued. She seemed withdrawn, though I often got the feeling she was coiling up, storing her venom until a future opportunity to sting me presented itself.

I was admittedly occupied with thoughts of Pierre. When I met Matilda for one of our post-fantasy talks, I immediately asked about him: would I see him again? Had he asked about me? But before she opened her mouth, I already knew she'd advise against seeing him again for fear that I'd reignite something. Because by this time, we were both aware my body was drawn to men my mind knew were not necessarily right for me.

"It's not that he's a bad man, Cassie," she said. "He's generous and intelligent. But he can also be dangerous to any woman who believes him to be capable of more intimacy than he is."

"If Pierre's so dangerous, why did you recruit him?"

"Because he was perfect for *that* particular fantasy. I was thrilled when he called me and said yes. We've been trying to recruit him for years. And I knew you wouldn't be disappointed. Isn't that the fantasy you wanted to experience?"

"Yes, I did. But—"

"No buts."

I nodded, on the brink of tears. *Oh God, I thought, don't cry. There's nothing to cry about. It was just a little fling. Some sex, great sex, but that's it.* Yet the tears flowed.

"Maybe I'm not cut out for this kind of thing," I said,

sniffling. I looked around Tracey's to see if any of the men, the ones watching the game on TV, the ones eating their po' boy sandwiches, had noticed. None had.

"Nonsense," Matilda said, handing me a tissue. "Have your feelings—they're normal ones. Pierre's a powerful man. Any woman would swoon. To be honest, I was almost hoping he wouldn't participate because there was a part of me that knew he'd have some kind of hold over you. But, Cassie, I can't stress this enough. This is a fantasy, and men who participate don't necessarily make great life partners. Cherish the moment and relish it, but let it go after."

I nodded and blew my nose.

A few weeks later, winter covered the city with a surprise frost. I stepped out into the chilly air, pulling the door to the Spinster Hotel shut behind me. I was going for a quick run before my shift, surprised all over again that New Orleans even had a winter. And this year, it was not a mild one. It was freezing, and featured the kind of chill that gets in your bones and makes you want to sit in a hot bathtub for hours to warm up. I wore a hat, mitts and thermal underwear, but it took me several blocks before the run did its job of heating me up.

I ran down Mandeville to Decatur and took a right to the French Market, avoiding the waterfront and port lands so as not to be reminded of Pierre, who owned almost all of it.

I wondered what he'd eventually do with all that vacant land. Build condos? Strip malls? Another casino? Will already grumbled about Marigny becoming "hipster heaven." Too many tourists flooded Frenchmen, he said, and not the good kind, not the ones with a true appreciation of music and food but rather the kind in the tacky party hats with the take-away plastic drink glasses, who haggled down the prices for artisan jewelry at the open-air market.

I ran past the long line at Café Du Monde. Though it was a major tourist attraction and one that most New Orleanians avoided, I loved ending a run with a Du Monde coffee. The beignets, I skipped. What's the point of running for forty minutes only to stop and eat a mountain of grease and sugar, Will always said. God, between Will and now Pierre, my mind was echoing with male voices. I had to shake them off.

When I returned home after my run, I was alarmed to find the front door open, even more alarmed to find Anna in the foyer of the Spinster Hotel, this time sifting through a large box wrapped in plain brown paper.

"Oh, Cassie, I'm so sorry," she said, the look of a nabbed thief on her face. "I accidentally opened your package. When I signed for it, I thought it was for me. I'm getting old. And my eyes . . . but it's a beautiful coat. And those shoes! Is this an early Christmas gift, my dear?"

I snatched the heavy box from her lap and examined the contents. Inside was a full-length camel coat with a simple tie. Next to it, a pair of black Christian Louboutin pumps with four-inch heels. I saw that Anna had opened the box, but not the card taped to the outside, thank goodness!

"It is a gift, Anna," I said, trying to hide my distress at her nosiness. This was no accident. She was increasingly curious about my comings and goings, the limo's presence a cause for concern every time it pulled up. Beside the coat and shoes there was also a small black velvet drawstring bag. Anna noticed it at the same time I did.

"What's in there?" she asked, pointing.

"Gloves," I said. I made up a lie about an assertive guy I had met at work whom I'd gone out with a couple of times and who was trying to woo me, adding in fake protest, "I wish he would stop buying me things. It's too soon."

"Nonsense!" she said. "Take it while you can."

Back in the safe confines of my own apartment, I opened the card attached to the box. Step Seven: *Curiosity.* How apt, I thought. Anna would pass with flying colors. Next, I opened the velvet bag. Had she seen what was in it, she might have fainted.

The next day, just after sunset, the limo pulled into the U-shaped driveway and deposited me directly in front of the Mansion. The previous time I had been here, the limo had pulled into the side entrance. This time the car came to a full stop at the grand front entrance. I had become accustomed to waiting for the driver to open the limo door for me, something a girl from Michigan could never have imagined before, and again he obliged. I stepped onto the cobblestones wearing the heels, which were, to my surprise, quite comfortable. Perhaps because they had cost a small fortune. Looking up at the house that night, I saw every room was ablaze with that same ocher glow, as though it was waiting for me before it could come alive again. An Arctic chill nipped at my bare ankles, and I was grateful for the full-length coat covering the rest of me.

I slowly ascended the wide marble stairs that lead to the front double doors, my stomach lurching at the thought of what tonight's fantasy would bring. I hoped that I had attained enough fearlessness, trust and confidence from the previous steps to really go through with this one. Those were the qualities I'd need to muster, Matilda told me. Plus, I needed something fulfilling and heady to push the final thoughts of Pierre out of my body, and Will out of my heart. I felt around in my pocket for the velvet bag. I had a feeling I'd accomplish both tonight.

Two knocks and Claudette greeted me in the foyer like an old acquaintance, falling short of the intimacy you'd use to meet a friend.

"I trust your ride here was comfortable?"

"It always is," I said, looking around the imposing entrance, taking in its beautifully curved staircase. I was grateful that the room was dim and warm, almost too warm, the heat coming from the parlor to my left where I could see a roaring fire. I noted the gold balustrade and plush red carpet running up the middle of the steps. The black-and-white floor tiles formed a spiral that culminated in a coat of arms inlaid in the center. The design featured a willow tree shading three nude women, each with a different skin tone—white, brown, black—under which were carved the words: *Nihil judicii. Nihil limitis. Nihil verecundiae.*

"What does that mean?" I asked Claudette.

"Our motto: No judgments. No limits. No shame."

"Right."

"Did you bring it?" she asked.

She didn't have to specify what "it" was. "Yes, I did." I pulled the velvet bag out of my pocket and handed it to her.

"It's time," she said, taking the bag from me and stepping behind me. I could hear her open the drawstring. Seconds later, she was securing a black satin blindfold across my eyes.

"Can you see anything?"

"No." And I couldn't. Just utter blackness. Claudette's hands were on my shoulders, pulling off my coat. And before I could even ask about what I was supposed to do next, I heard her quietly pad away.

For several minutes, I stood there, hardly moving. The only sounds I could hear were the crackling of the fire, the clack of my heels as I nervously shifted my weight from one leg to the other and the tinkle of my bracelet every time I moved my arm. I was grateful the room was so warm, because apart from my blindfold and heels, I wasn't wearing a thing. The Step card had specified that I should bring the velvet bag in my pocket and arrive wearing *only* the camel coat and heels. I stood for what felt like forever blindfolded and naked, waiting for the fantasy to begin.

After a while, I found that without sight, my other senses became heightened. At one point I was certain someone was in the foyer with me even though I hadn't heard anyone enter. I could just sense a presence, one that sent a slight shiver down my spine.

"Is anyone here?" I asked. "Please say something." There were no words, but a few seconds later, I heard breathing.

"Someone *is* here," I said. Despite the intense heat, I began to shiver out of nervousness. "What do you want me to do?"

I heard a man clear his throat, which caused me to jump.

"Who are you?" I asked, a little too loudly. I was blindfolded, not deaf, but for some reason my voice projected more than usual.

"Make a quarter turn to your left," the voice said. "Take five steps and stop."

It had a very sexy timbre, maybe belonging to a man who was a little older, perhaps someone used to being in charge. I did as instructed, sensing I was heading towards this voice.

"Please put your hands out." I did so. "Now walk forward until you touch me."

There was something about the languidness in his voice that pulled me forward. I took one, then two careful steps, aware how blindness can seriously throw off your balance. I stretched out my hands until they made contact with toned, warm flesh. Though I didn't have the nerve to let my hands trail down, I got the sense that he was naked, too, and tall, with a taut, broad chest.

"Cassie, do you accept the Step?"

His voice was like liquid smoke, his *s*'s curling around the vowels.

"Yes, I do," I said, with a little too much enthusiasm perhaps, as I finally let my hands trail down the sides of his lean torso and back up his stomach to his collarbone. I realized that my shyness was gone, it had melted, or I had left it somewhere at Halo, or maybe in the middle of the Gulf, or perhaps in the back of a limo. I didn't know, couldn't remember, and didn't care.

"What's your name?" I asked.

"It doesn't matter, Cassie. May I?"

"May you what?"

"Touch your skin?"

I dropped my hands to my sides, as willing as I'd ever been to submit. I nodded as he stepped so close to me I could feel his fingers brush my nipples, which were already responding. He moved his hands slowly, artfully, across my breasts, cupping one and taking it into his cool, wet mouth. His other arm wrapped around me, lingering at my buttocks and pulling me into him so that our bodies were pressed skin to skin. I could feel him hard against my thigh. His hand slid behind me and up. I was already wet.

I remembered how in the beginning it had taken a while for my body to respond, but now, my passion was instant. I wanted him. No, not him. How could I want *him*, a man I didn't even know? But I wanted *this*. All of *this*. And I began to understand what Matilda meant when she said that if I could get back into my body, I could move thoughts of Pierre out of my head. Then, just as quickly as things had begun, the man released me from his hot embrace and I almost tipped over on my heels.

"Where are you?" I asked, my hands reaching into the air around me. "Where did you go?"

"Follow my voice, Cassie."

It was now coming from the other side of the foyer. I turned slightly to follow it. We were moving away from the fire, away from the warmth of the parlor to another room, a different room.

"That's right, one foot in front of the other," he whispered. "Do you know how sexy you look wearing just those heels?"

His words were making me hotter and wetter, as I carefully made my way towards his voice, my arms out in front of me. I felt the warmth of another fire on the front of my body. When I felt carpet under my heels, I almost tripped.

"There's a chair right in front of you. Two more steps." My fingers hit a highback wooden chair, which felt as big as a throne. I took a seat on what felt like a raw silk cushion. I felt self-conscious of what my stomach looked like in a seated position. I pressed my legs together. *Stop it, Cassie. Now's not the time to think.* The silk felt lovely under my butt, though, and my hands began stroking the fabric. I could sense the man moving around the room until he was directly behind my chair.

I felt his large, warm hands on my shoulders, caressing my skin. They trailed up my neck, where he left one hand cradling the back of my neck, while the other fetched something in front of us. The rim of a glass grazed my lips, and my nose was hit with the warm, full-bodied smell of red wine.

"Take a sip, Cassie."

He gently tipped the glass forward. I took an eager gulp. I was no connoisseur, but the wine tasted rich and layered. I don't know if I tasted oak or cherry or chocolate tones, but I knew it was probably the most expensive wine I had ever swallowed. I heard him gently place the glass back on the table. Seconds later he moved in front of me and his mouth was on mine, his tongue searching. He tasted like wine, too, and chocolate. Every cell inside me came alive to his taste and touch, smell and feel. Then he stopped.

"Are you hungry, Cassie?"

I nodded.

"What are you hungry for?"

"You."

"That's later. First, open that delicious mouth of yours."

I did so and he began rubbing morsels of fruit across my lips, leaving me just enough time to smell them and then reach out my tongue for a delicate taste. I tasted the juicy flesh of a mango, and when my tongue curled around a small slice that he proffered with his fingers, I licked them both. Then he fed me some strawberries, one after the other, some dipped in chocolate, others in cream. But it was the truffles that sent me over the edge; he only allowed me to lick and nibble at the edges, never letting me have a full bite. After each swallow, he pressed his mouth to mine, kissing me. I couldn't see his face, but the sensation was excruciating, the way he urged my mouth open with his tongue.

Then he was straddling my legs, standing over me as I lay back in my cushioned throne. I could feel his naked thighs against the outside of mine. I gulped as he grabbed the chair's wooden arms, jerking it forward.

"Hold your hands out," he said, and when I did, I came in contact with him, firm, warm and soft.

I wrapped a hand around him, eagerly bringing him to my mouth. Using both hands, I took him in deeper, feeling the pleasure I was giving, of pleasing, coming over me again. I imagined what I must look like in this chair, blindfolded, in heels, with this beautiful body over me. A tingle passed through me at the thought.

"Stop, Cassie," he said, easing back from my mouth. "That feels amazing, but you have to stop."

He lifted me off the seat and onto my feet. My limbs were wobbly with desire. Standing behind me, he walked me forward a few feet, placing my hands on what I thought was the arm of a silk divan. I took in the smell of oranges and wine and vanilla candles. I could hear the fire spit and spark in front of us, and my heart raced. My back arched as I felt his hands firmly grasp both sides of my hips, tugging me back towards him. I could feel his desire for me, and he hardened and stiffened more.

"I'm going to put myself inside you now, Cassie. Do you want that?"

I lifted up to him, to show him that yes, I wanted this, very much.

"Tell me, Cassie. Say it."

"I want you," I whispered, my voice choked the feeling.

"Say it, Cassie. Tell me you want it."

"I do! I want it!"

"Say it!"

"I want you. I want you inside me. *Now!*" I commanded.

I heard him ripping open a packet, and seconds later, I felt all of him slide into me, plunging deep and fast and hard. I felt him reach around and under me, his fingers touching me in a dazzling rhythm. His other held my hip so firmly he was practically lifting me up off the floor. He gathered a fistful of my hair and tugged my head gently backwards. His hands trailed down my arched back, finally grabbing my buttocks and kneading them with an intensity that sent me spinning. His low growls made me feel like I was driving him mad.

"You look so hot with your ass in the air like this, Cassie. I love it. Do you?"

"Yes."

"Say it. Say it louder."

"I love it . . . I love fucking you like this," I said, surprising myself with the words. It felt animalistic but so divine.

He spread my legs open wider, and began moving harder and faster.

"Oh God," I said. It was all happening at once and so fast, desire gathering a storm inside me.

"You can come now. I want you to come, Cassie," he urged, and that's what I did, full-bodied and wholeheartedly. Then he followed. And when he was done, he pulled away and I lay forward across the divan, so completely spent that I slid gently onto the bearskin rug and lay there on my back. I felt him slide down next to me. I went to lift my blindfold.

"Don't," he said, grabbing my hand, keeping the blind-fold intact.

"But I want to see you. I want to look at the face capable of doing that to my body."

"I value my anonymity."

Sensing my frustration, he leaned towards my face and took my hand in his.

"Here, feel my face," he offered. "But leave the blind-fold on."

He took my hand and brought it to his slightly stubbly cheek. I felt a sharp, angular jaw, wide-set eyes, soft hair, longish, with sideburns at the temple. My fingers caressed a wide mouth, and he playfully bit them. Then my hand moved once more down his muscular chest and across his taut stomach.

"You feel amazing," I said.

"Right back at you . . . But it's time for me to go, Cassie. Before I do, open your hand."

I did so and felt him press a small round coin—my Step Seven charm, *Curiosity*—into my damp palm. It felt more

delicate and fragile when I couldn't see it, like the slightest
squeeze would crush it.

"Thank you," I said, my body still vibrating. I listened to
him pad away towards the exit.

Seconds later, he whispered his goodbye.

"Bye," I said.

After he shut the door quietly behind him, I pulled off
the blindfold and looked around the room. It was stunning,
masculine, a big oak desk in the middle and wall-to-wall
books on three sides. The thick sandalwood candles flickered on the table, where a big bowl of oranges rested. I sat
there naked, fingers combing through the hairs of the plush
bearskin rug on which I lay. The fire gradually dwindled.

As I secured my Step Seven charm to my bracelet, I wondered what he had looked like, my new, mysterious man, the
one who had gone just moments before, leaving me sated
and curious, and fully alive to myself.

XI

After my blindfold fantasy, life seemed more vivid. All of my senses were alive. I paid greater attention to the things and people I used to ignore. As I walked, I'd let my hands trail the gates in the Garden District, noticing the cornhusks or the little birds carved into the wrought iron, imagining the artist creating those ornamental touches. It used to irritate me when our regulars at the Café would take up a table outside, order one coffee and spend the morning chatting with everyone walking by, clogging the narrow sidewalk with dogs and bikes. Now I marveled at the early morning intimacy of Frenchmen Street, how people from different races and ages all convened around the same table at the Café. I felt lucky to be a part of this community. I began, in fact, to feel at home.

Instead of just plopping his coffee in front of him, I asked the chatty old man with the fancy carved walking stick some questions about his life. He told me about a wife who ran off with his lawyer and the three daughters he rarely saw. I began to understand that this man's eccentricities were probably meant to draw people to him, so he could talk and feel less lonely. And with a little encouragement, Tim from Michael's bike shop a few doors down told me some harrowing tales about surviving the hurricanes, and about some friends who didn't make it. "Many survived the hurricane only to die of heartbreak after it," he said.

And I believed him, knowing that loss and disappointment can create such pain.

New Orleans was experiencing one of the warmest winters on record, so when a volunteer called to tell me I had won the Revitalization Ball's raffle for a trip for two to Whistler, British Columbia, for the weekend, I was excited. I wanted to ski again, but mostly I needed to feel a real winter on my skin. Though I embraced the South and was beginning to know the city in my bones, I was a Northern girl at heart.

Before leaving for my trip, I asked Anna to keep Dixie for the week in her apartment downstairs. I didn't want to give her access to my place in case she snooped around and found my fantasy journal, or any other evidence that explained those mysterious limo rides. When I told Matilda about my prize and that I'd be away, beyond telling me to have fun and to get in touch when I was back, she didn't say much.

Will was a little reluctant to give me the time off, but there was always a short post-holiday lull before Mardi Gras kicked in. I reminded him that this was the perfect time for me to take vacation days.

"I guess," he said after I told him. He'd joined me outside

for a quick coffee after the breakfast crowd left. "Are you going alone?"

"I don't really have anyone I could go with."

"What about Pierre Castille?" He practically spat out the name.

"Oh, please," I said, hopefully camouflaging the shudder I felt at hearing "Pierre" spoken out loud. "That was nothing. In every sense of the word."

"You cast a spell on him, Cassie. Has he been in touch?" Will made no attempt to hide his jealousy, which now hovered over our metal patio table like a bit of sullen weather.

"No, Will, he has not. Nor do I expect him to," I said, meaning it. I ran the hem of my apron through my fingers, thinking how wildly curious I was about Will's connection to Pierre. I finally got up the nerve to ask.

"So, how well do you know Pierre exactly? And why had you never mentioned him before?"

"Holy Cross," he said, referring to a private school for boys. "I went on scholarship. His dad pulled some strings to get me in."

"So you were friends as kids?"

"Best friends. For years. But time and temperament pulled us apart. Then this place put a nail in the coffin," he said, pointing to the condominium across the street. "His father built Castille Development, and the Castilles built that monstrosity. I fought against it. I lost. Don't know why it had to be nine stories. Four, maybe five, but they built a fucking high-rise on Frenchmen. How can city council allow that but not allow me to have a couple dozen people eating dinner and having drinks upstairs at Café Rose?"

"Well, there is the matter of the aging beams. And also the sixty-year-old electrical wiring."

"I would fix those things, Cassie, I would," he said, then took a sip of his coffee.

"With the money you were going to donate when you bid on me at the ball?" I said.

He winced at the memory, and I was sorry to have brought it up.

"I was momentarily swept up in the proceedings." Then, quickly changing the subject, he added, "I'd take out a loan to do the renos. I might even qualify for an improvement grant. Or one of those hurricane funds, maybe. I need to figure out a way to earn more money from this goddamn building."

I glanced across the street at the nine-story, blond-brick building, thinking that every time Will looked at it, he probably thought of Pierre.

"I'll miss you, Cassie."

I couldn't believe I'd heard what I just heard. "It's just four days."

"I didn't know you skied."

"It's been a while. Ten years," I said, reminded that my old skiwear was probably horribly out of date. "You ever ski?"

"Nope. Southern boy born and bred. I'm still amazed by snow, when we get it. Take pictures, will you?" he asked. Then adopting the deepest of Southern accents, he added, "'Cause I ain't never seen no big mountains 'afore in my *en*-tire life!"

Staring up at Whistler Mountain three weeks later, center-ing it through a viewfinder for a photograph, I had to admit I'd never seen a mountain this big either. In Michigan we skied on hills—high ones, steep ones, but hills nonetheless. They had names like Mount Brighton and Mount Holly, but they weren't full-on mountains. Not like this. Despite the fact that it was a clear day, I couldn't even see the top, and yet for January it wasn't nearly as cold here in British Columbia as Michigan winters could get. In fact, I began to curse my brand-new baby-blue one-piece suit because I had to unzip the jacket and let it collapse around my waist to get some relief from the heat generated by the beating sun. I was sure I looked like an oddly colored tulip with wilted petals. My white toque and white mitts soon became dotted with coffee and hot chocolate because it took a day and a half of pacing at the foot of the mountain before I got the nerve to take the chair to the top.

I'd spent some time in Canada, in Windsor, Ontario, in particular, because the drinking age was lower than Michigan's and I was dating Scott, a man who drank a lot even before I married him. I remember for a while trying to keep up with him, but I just didn't like the effects of all that alcohol on my body. Still, it was the hallmark of our court-ship that everything Scott did and liked, I would find myself doing and liking as well. He drove Fords, and so a Focus was my first car. He liked Thai food, so I became a fan myself. Scott was an avid skier, so I became one too. But skiing was about the only thing he introduced me to that I actually liked and eventually became pretty good at.

At first we skied together, Scott never more in his element than when he was telling or showing me how to do something. But I was a willing partner, *so* wanting it to work, for us to bond and click, that I risked breaking my neck on moguls after only three days of lessons. I was a natural, something that pleased Scott at first and then slowly began to bother him. Eventually, while I'd hit the slopes in the morning, Scott would stay back and keep a couch warm in front of the fire and a brandy ready for when I returned. Skiing alone, I felt a sense of independence and the thrill that comes from courting adrenaline rushes. I loved going fast and the feel of my thigh muscles working hard in the cold. But this newfound hobby was short-lived. Once Scott saw that I was actually enjoying myself, and sometimes even drawing a bit of male attention my way, we stopped skiing altogether.

Now, trudging through Whistler's crowded main square in my new ski outfit, I felt some bad déjà vu, but also some good. Before Scott got sicker, I had to admit some of our happiest days as a couple were spent on those weekend trips to the Upper Peninsula. Maybe this is what it felt like to begin forgiving Scott, to let go of my resentment towards him and his selfish decisions, the ones that had left me a widow at twenty-nine. I hoped so. I was done blaming him for my aloneness, done feeling sad about it. And on days like today, when the sun was bright and the snow was sparkling, I could even say I loved my life more because it was finally, completely my own. I looked up at the mountain. I would never take this kind of beauty for granted, even if I lived here and saw this every single day. It wasn't just gratitude that flooded my heart at that moment, but unadulterated joy.

"Here, let me take a picture of you in front of the mountain."

I was startled by the voice and the hand, which before I could protest was wrapping around my camera.

"Whoa!" I said, pulling it away. It took me a couple of seconds to take in the young man with a dimple in his left cheek, and the shaggy brown hair peeking out from under his black toque. I detected a slight French accent.

"I wasn't trying to take it," he said, his palms open to me in surrender. Then he smiled, his teeth bright white against his sun-kissed face. "I thought you'd like to be in the picture. My name is Theo."

"Hi," I said, cautiously offering a hand, the other one still holding my camera out of his reach. He couldn't have been more than thirty years old. But this was a face that basked in sun and wind all day. The sexy wrinkles around brown eyes gave him a patina of maturity despite his youth. "Cassie."

"And I'm sorry. I didn't mean to scare you. I work here. I'm a ski instructor."

Hmm. I had been alone for two days, and I'd enjoyed those days a lot. But here was this gorgeous man in front of me. In all likelihood he was one of Matilda's. I decided to cut to the chase.

"So you work here, in Whistler? Or are you one of the . . . *you know . . . ?*"

He cocked his head at my question.

"One of the . . . you-know-*whats?* . . . One of the . . . *men?*"

He glanced around the crowded village square, a confused look on his face. "Well, I am . . . a *man,*" he said, clearly drawing a blank.

It occurred to me then that he could be just a guy, a random guy, someone very cute who happened to come up to talk to me, someone with no relation to S.E.C.R.E.T. at all. This seemed less impossible to imagine, and I smiled at that thought.

"Okay," I said. "Now *I'm* sorry. And I didn't mean to assume you were a camera thief." I was participating in the Canadian pastime of apologizing to strangers, something referred to in my guidebook.

"How about a free ski lesson to make it up to me?" the man offered. Yes, there definitely was a slight French accent—or rather, Québécois.

"What if I don't need a lesson?" I said, feeling a little confidence return.

"So you're familiar with these slopes?" He smiled an irresistible smile. "You know the conditions and can spot the black diamond runs, know which lifts take you where, and which beginner runs turn treacherous if you're not paying attention?" Who was I kidding?

"No, actually," I admitted. "I've been circling the base for a couple of days. I don't know if I have the nerve to go up."

"I'll be your nerve," he said, giving me his arm.

⁓

Theo was a natural teacher, and though I resisted the scarier black diamond runs, after an hour of easily carving up the Saddle, the cold glacial slope where the snow is as sharp and crisp as I'd ever known snow to be, we took an express lift to the Symphony Bowl. Theo promised me a mix of challenging drops with easy ridges to give my quivering thigh muscles a bit of a break, then a leisurely five-mile run to the village. I was glad for my nightly running routine in New Orleans. Had I hit the slopes with no prior conditioning, I'd have been paralytic in front of a fire for the rest of the weekend.

At the rim of the Bowl, I had to stop. Yes, the white rippled snow, which stretched to meet a sky so blue it hurt to look at it, was utterly breathtaking. But I also marveled at how my world had changed with a simple "yes." Over the last several months, I had been able to do things that would have been utterly inconceivable a year ago. Not just the sex with strangers, but volunteering for the Ball, taking up running, dressing a little sexier, being more outgoing with people, standing up for myself, and now, coming here, alone, with little idea of how my four days would unfold.

L . M A R I E   A D E L I N E

I never would have done these things before accepting the gift of S.E.C.R.E.T.

When this young man balancing skis on his shoulder had approached me in the square, instead of recoiling from the advance, or questioning it, I tried to accept that this was possible, that I might be worthy of this man's attention. An hour later, quite literally on top of the world, I began to feel transformed. Yet there was still part of me that doubted the spontaneity. Part of me was still waiting for us to reach a crest and share a lingering look, and for Theo to ask if I'd accept the Step.

"Beautiful," Theo muttered, stopping next to me and taking in the view I was admiring.

"I know. I don't think I've seen anything this spectacular in my entire life."

"I meant you," he said, and I caught a glimpse of his casual grin, before he pushed off and dropped over the lip of the Bowl.

I couldn't help but follow him down, and for a few terrifying seconds I was airborne. After a wobbly landing, I righted myself and fell into the groove he'd carved ahead of me. He expertly weaved through the glades, glancing back every once in a while to make sure I was keeping up. After a hard right turn at an unmarked path, we soon joined a cluster of skiers beating dusk to the cozy village, now twinkling yellow and pink in the fading sun.

At the base we skied up to each other, and he held up a hand for a high-five.

"Brave girl!" he said.

"What was so brave?" I asked as our gloved hands made contact. I felt flushed and giddy from the fast trip down.

"The first mile of that last run was a black diamond run and you just did it. Without even thinking!"

I felt something like pride mingled with glee.

"A drink to celebrate?" I asked.

We made our way to Chateau Whistler, where I was staying, and crossed the Great Hall, where everyone seemed to know Theo. He introduced me to the waiter, Marcel, an old friend also from Québec, who brought us fondue and two hot rum toddies, followed by steaming bowls of mussels and frites. I was so hungry I began devouring handfuls of fries, then caught myself.

"Oh my God," I said, mortified. "I'm eating like an animal. Look at me," I said, unable to resist popping another handful into my mouth.

"That's what I've been doing all day," he said, reaching across the table and pulling me towards him for a kiss. His hands were strong and callused from gripping ski poles all day. His hair was tousled and I knew mine was too, though probably not so adorably. But it didn't matter. This guy was into me, I could tell. I flashed back to Pauline and her man in Café Rose, and their intense connection. Now I was having the same sort of experience. I shyly glanced around the chalet to see if anyone was noticing this . . . me . . . *us*. No. We were in our own private world, even in public.

We talked for a long time after that, mostly about skiing and the feeling it gave us, reliving for each other our finest moments from that day. I wasn't avoiding any personal questions. They just didn't seem as important as the way he was touching my wrist or looking into my eyes. After dinner, when he snatched the bill off the table and stood looking down at me, holding out his hand, I knew we weren't going to say good-night anytime soon.

⌒

I hadn't even realized how bone-chilled I was until Theo peeled my clothes off in the bathroom of my hotel room, one layer after the other.

"Is there some flesh underneath all of this?" he joked as he pulled off my leggings.

"Yes." I laughed.

"Promise?"

"Promise."

After he'd flung my clothes in a pile just outside the bathroom, I was completely naked except for a few impressive bruises blooming on my calves and arms. Those elicited a long slow whistle from Theo.

"Wow, war wounds." He turned on the shower and steam started to fill the room. "Time to warm you up."

"You're not making me go in there on my own, are you?" I asked, more shocked by my boldness than he seemed to be.

He laughed, ripping off his clothes. His body was fit

and athletic. Yes, this man skied all day. All year, probably. I stepped into the shower and he joined me, and seconds later our mouths met under the gushing water. He trailed his hands down my arms, guiding my hands up over my head and pushing them against the wet wall behind us. He used his knees to coax mine open, lifting my body slightly so my legs were on either side of him. He was firm but not forceful. I felt like a starfish pressed against the wall. He licked down the side of my neck, his hardness against my stomach. Then he gathered one of my breasts in his wide hand and sucked the droplets of water off my nipple. The fingers of his other hand began an aching descent down my body, until he slipped one, then another, inside. I could feel my own wetness while the water pummeled us. He locked eyes with me, and I brought my arms down and entwined my hands in his wet hair. The water was making my feet slip, so he gently placed one hand behind my buttocks, anchoring me there.

"You like this?"

"I've never done this before," I said.

"Want to try something new, then?"

The steam in the shower was building around us. I could feel all the pores of my skin opening to him, all of me opening to him.

"I'd try anything with you," I said.

He lifted my naked body around his hips, and before I knew it he was carrying me, dripping, out of the bathroom and across the tile and then the carpet to the king-size bed, where he laid me down. He returned to the bathroom to shut the shower off and to find his pants, digging into his pockets, I assumed, for a condom. Then he stood at the edge of the bed, glistening.

I crawled towards him, taking him into my mouth while he watched. Seconds later, he ripped open the package and handed me the condom. I unfurled it over him, and then he gently pushed me down onto my back and licked me expertly, eagerly, my knees splayed open, an arm flung across my eyes. Before I could even catch my breath, he turned me over in his strong arms, so my back was to his front, and I could feel his erection harder than it had been even a few minutes before.

Kissing down the side of my neck, he whispered, "We're just getting started." Nudging my legs apart, he pulled one of my thighs over the top of his, until our bodies formed an entwined letter S. I felt his hands exploring my back, and then exploring a whole new part of me. At first it was just a finger, painful at first, but the pain quickly subsided and gave way to a wide, delicious fullness. I felt my stomach drop the same thrilling way it did when I skied over the ridge. Then he entered me from behind, not in the way I was expecting. The feeling was intensely, excruciatingly pleasurable. He clutched me hard to keep me close to him.

"Is it okay? Are you okay?" he whispered, tenderly combing my wet hair away from my face and neck.

"Yes," I said. "Yes. It feels so . . . it's a good hurt."

"I can stop anytime. You sure it feels good?"

I nodded again, because it did, it felt so good, and so intimate, this thing we were doing. I clutched a fistful of the sheets and pulled them to me as the full sensation gave way to a wave of intense pleasure that moved through my whole body. This was something I would never in a million years have thought I'd want to try. But here I was saying "yes, yes, yes" as he inched inside me even deeper and brought his hand around and under me, making me wetter and wetter. I came again, pushing backwards into him, the abandon I felt hard to contain. I needed this kind of release, in this place, in this room, in this bed, with this man who seemed put here to take me through this experience.

"I'm going to come. You're making me come now," he said, clutching my center with one hand, bending me farther forward as he bit softly into my shoulder, his other hand caressing my breasts. When he was done, he subsided with the gentlest tug and we both shifted onto our backs, his hand across my stomach, to look at the ornate ceiling that neither of us had noticed until just then.

"That was . . . intense," he said.

"I know," I said, still gasping for air.

I had done something new and it was thrilling, but now I was feeling a bit vulnerable. This man wasn't from S.E.C.R.E.T. There had been no Step to accept, just a plunge into all-new terrain. Theo must have sensed my shift in mood. "You okay?"

"I am. I just . . . I've never done that in my life. I don't normally pick up strangers and take them to bed," I said.

Despite the fact that the men from S.E.C.R.E.T. were technically strangers, the women from S.E.C.R.E.T. knew them.

"So what if you did? Where's the crime in that?"

"I guess I never saw myself as that kind of woman."

"I see that kind of woman as daring, brave."

"Really? You see me like that?"

"I do," he said, gently spooning me in a way that was so tender, it was odd to think we barely knew one another. He pulled a heavy duvet over our bodies and nested it around us.

When I woke six hours later, he was gone. And oddly, I was fine with that. I was so happy to have had those moments with him, and to let them pass without feeling loss. As sweet as he was, I actually wanted to enjoy my last days in Whistler alone. Still, it was nice to read a note he left on the bathroom vanity: *Cassie, you are lovely. And I am late for work! But you know where to find me. À bientôt, Theo.*

Matilda was admiring my pictures as I yammered on in the coach house about how exciting it had been to hit the slopes again. I told her about the mini-moguls on Blackcomb Mountain, where I spent my last day. Danica came over to us with coffees and cooed over a photo Marcel had taken of Theo and me enjoying our fondue.

"He is keee-yoot," she said, before ducking away and leaving Matilda and me alone.

When I had told her about Theo, she was delighted. She asked me how we met, what he said, what I said. Then I told her about . . . what we did.

"Did you enjoy it?" she asked.

"Yes," I said. "I'd do it again, maybe. With the right partner. Someone I could trust."

"Cassie, I have something for you," she said, opening a drawer in the desk and pulling out a small wooden box.

She opened the box. The Step Eight charm looked dazzling against its black velvet background.

"But, I thought Theo was just some random guy, not a participant."

"It doesn't matter if he was part of our society or not."

"I don't understand."

"This Step is *Bravery*, which is different from courage because bravery requires you take risks without overthinking things. *Bravery* says, 'Go for it.' So, whether or not Theo is part of S.E.C.R.E.T. is irrelevant. You've earned this charm."

I plucked the charm from the box, turned it over in my hand and then clicked it into place on my bracelet. I gave my wrist a shake and admired the twinkling charms. So was Theo a random stranger drawn to me naturally? Or was he involved in S.E.C.R.E.T? I couldn't figure it out. But perhaps Matilda was right: it didn't matter.

"I'll allow myself to believe I attracted Theo," I said, "Though I still have my doubts."

"Good, Cassie. No more being a wallflower. You, my dear, have blossomed."

XII

For the weeks leading up to Mardi Gras, the whole city of New Orleans takes on the spirit of a bride making last-minute preparations for her big day. No matter that the festivities take place this year, and next year, and every year, each Mardi Gras feels like the last, best one.

When I first moved here, I was fascinated by the krewes, the groups, some ancient, some modern, that put on the balls and built the floats for Mardi Gras parades. Mostly, I wondered why you'd spend so much of your spare time sewing costumes and gluing sequins. But after living here for a few years I began to understand the fatalistic nature of the average New Orleanian. People in this city tend to live and love vividly for today.

Even if I had wanted to join a krewe, many of the older ones—with names like Proteus, Rex and Bacchus—were downright impossible to get into, unless your bloodline was that of Bayou royalty. But nearing the end of my time with S.E.C.R.E.T., I began to feel that strong tug to belong to someone or something—which is, after all, the only anti-dote to loneliness. I was starting to see that melancholy isn't romantic. It's just a prettier word for *depression.*

In the month before Mardi Gras, I couldn't walk down a street in Marigny or Tremé, let alone the French Quarter, without envying those sewing circles gathered on a porch, hand-stitching sparkly costumes and securing sequins to elaborate masks or sky-high feathered headdresses. Other nights, I'd take a run through the Warehouse District and spot, through a crack in a door, spray-painters in masks putting the finishing touches on a vivid float. My heart would skip a beat and I was able to let in a little joy.

But there was one event that struck my heart with sheer, unadulterated terror: the annual Les Filles de Frenchmen Revue, a Mardi Gras burlesque show featuring the women who worked at the bars and restaurants in Marigny. It was considered a sexy way for our neighborhood to celebrate, and every year Tracina, one of the lead organizers, perfunc-torily asked if I wanted to participate. Every year I said no. Unequivocally no. Will allowed Les Filles to use the second floor of the Café to rehearse their dances, never failing to mention that if twenty girls can stomp around upstairs without falling through the ancient floorboards, surely twenty customers quietly sitting and eating wouldn't pose any danger either.

This year, not only did Tracina fail to ask me to partici-pate, she also bowed out of the revue herself, citing family obligations. Will told me her brother's condition was getting more complicated to deal with as he hit adolescence, some-thing I tried then to keep in mind whenever I was on the cusp of criticizing her.

I was surprised when Will put the gears to me about joining Les Filles.

"Come on, Cassie. Who's going to represent Café Rose at the Revue?"

"Dell. She has really nice legs," I said, avoiding eye con-tact with him while wiping down the coffee station.

"But—"

"No. That's my final answer." I dumped the tray of empty milk cartons into the trash to punctuate my decision.

"Coward," Will teased.

"I'll have you know, Mr. Foret, that I've done a few things this year that would set your teeth chattering. It just so hap-pens that I know the limits of my courage. And that means *not* shaking my tits at a crowd of drunk men."

The night of the Revue, I was closing the Café for Tracina for the second time that week. At eight o'clock sharp, while turning over the chairs to do the mopping, I heard the danc-ers upstairs practicing one last time—a dozen graceful ponies set loose above my head. I could hear each "Fille" perform her individual routine for the group to raucous laughter, hooting and whistling. Those familiar feelings of loneliness and inferiority returned to me then, along with the thought that I'd be ridiculed if I ever attempted such a thing. At thirty-five, almost thirty-six, I'd be the oldest dancer next to Steamboat Betty and Kit DeMarco. Kit was a bartender from the Spotted Cat, who at forty-one could still pull off a blue pixie hair-do and denim cutoffs. Steamboat Betty manned the antique cigarette booth at Snug Harbor and performed every year wearing the same burlesque outfit she claimed to have worn for thirty-six years in a row, never failing to boast that it still—sort of—fit her. Plus, there was no way I could dance next to Angela Rejean, a statuesque Haitian goddess who worked as a hostess at Maison and was a jazz singer on the side. Her body was so perfect that it made being jealous kind of pointless.

After completing my shut-down duties, I headed upstairs to hand the keys to Kit, who had offered to lock up after they were done. The review didn't start until after 10 p.m. The girls would rehearse up until the last minute, and in the meantime, I wanted to go home and shower off the day. I had hoped to see Will at the show, but earlier in the day, when I asked him if he and Tracina were going to attend the event, he had shrugged noncommittally.

At the top of the stairs, I stepped past a new girl, with blond corkscrew curls, sitting cross-legged on the floor holding a hand-mirror. She was applying false eyelashes with expert precision. I couldn't tell if her hair was a wig or real, but it was mesmerizing. A dozen more girls in various stages of undress were sitting or standing about, all getting ready for the big night, coats piled on the old mattress Will kept on the floor and sometimes slept on. Besides the mattress, the only other furniture up here was a broken wooden chair, which I'd sometimes find Will straddling, lost in thought, his chin resting on the back. The Café was a big empty space, perfect for a temporary rehearsal room. We closed early, were only a few doors down from the Blue Nile, which was hosting the event this year, and the bathroom upstairs was brand-new, though still lacking a door. Several women, one topless, were craning around the bathroom mirror, taking turns applying stage makeup. Curling irons and hair straighteners were plugged in everywhere. Bright costumes, feather boas and masks added festivity to the usually dull, gray room.

I found Kit, in a strapless bra and stockings, tapping out a dance sequence, her costume hanging on the exposed brick wall like a piece of art. She had had it specially made, a white lace bodice on a black satin backdrop, with scalloped pink trim around the sweetheart-cut frontpiece. The laces up the back were pink too. I reached out to touch it, but shuddered when my fingers brushed the satin, memories of being blindfolded returning to me in a hot rush. I could never pull off what Kit and the rest of the girls were about to do in front of a room full of people—not without a blindfold.

"Hey, Cass. Make sure you thank Will for letting us stay after closing. I'll get the keys back to you at the Blue Nile," she said, not missing a beat with her feet. "You're coming tonight, right?"

"I never miss it."

"You should dance with us one year, Cassie," yelled Angela from the cluster of girls crowding the washroom.

I felt flattered by her attention, but said, "I'd make a total fool of myself."

"You're *supposed* to make a fool of yourself. That's what makes it sexy," she crooned.

The other women laughed and nodded while Kit gave me a little shake of her behind. "Do dykes normally dress like this?" Kit asked me teasingly.

When she came out a couple of years ago, the only person who was surprised was Will. "Typical hetero," Tracina had said, rolling her eyes at him. "Just because she dresses sexy, you think it's all for male attention."

Kit had begun dressing sexier after she came out and got a steady girlfriend. And tonight she had drawn a mole by her mouth and was wearing false eyelashes and the reddest shade of lipstick I'd ever seen. She'd grown the blue pixie cutout into a longer, very attractive shag. Still, her exaggerated girlishness contrasted with her trademark cowboy boots and the black terry-cloth sweatbands that she always wore around both wrists.

"Maybe I'll join you guys next year, Kit," I said, kind of meaning it.

"Promise?"

"No." I laughed.

I wished the girls luck and ducked down the stairs, but at the bottom, I realized that I had forgotten to hand Kit the keys! As I turned to run back up, I smashed headlong into Kit herself, who was heading down, probably having had the same realization. Instead of bouncing off me, she completely lost her footing and slid down the last five steps, landing butt first on the hard tile floor. Luckily, I was wearing sneakers.

"Kit!"

"Jesus crap," she groaned, rolling over onto her side.

"Are you okay?"

"I think I broke my ass!"

I clambered down the remaining steps to her. "Oh my God! I'm so sorry! Let me help you!"

By then Angela, in four-inch stilettos, was making her way carefully down, a bright pink boa draped over her shoulders and wrapped around her wrists.

Kit lay perfectly still. "Don't move me, Ange. Oh. This isn't good. It's not my ass. It's my tailbone."

"Oh dear!" Angela cried, crouching over her. "Can you sit up? Can you feel your legs? Are you seeing double? Who am I? Who is the president? Should I call an ambulance?"

Without waiting for a reply, Angela made her unsteady way to the kitchen phone. I watched Kit attempt to right herself, wince, and lay back down.

"Cassie," she whispered.

I crawled closer. "What is it, Kit?"

"Cassie . . . this floor . . . is *really* dirty."

"I know. I'm sorry," I said. I was about to take her hand to console her, when I noticed her fall had caused one of her wristbands to shift, exposing a portion of a shiny gold bracelet—a S.E.C.R.E.T. bracelet! Covered in charms!

A look passed between us.

"What the—?"

"My ass is just fine, Cassie. And one more thing," Kit whispered, crooking her finger to bring me closer. I leaned towards her lipsticked mouth. "Do you . . . accept your final Step?"

"Do I *what*? With *you*? I mean, you're adorable and every-thing, Kit, but—"

A smile played across her lips as she sat up. "Relax, I'm not a participant. But I have been asked to nudge you for-ward. You're almost there, girl. Now's not the time to back down. Not when it's about to get *really* fun!"

When we heard Angela returning from the kitchen, Kit collapsed back to the floor, fake-groaning all over again.

"This is a problem," Angela said, hands on her hips.

"I know. I mean, who will dance in my place?" Kit asked, an arm dramatically flung over her eyes. "Who can we get on such short notice?"

"I don't know," said Angela.

Was she in on this too?

"I mean, who do we know who's free tonight? And cute? And could *totally fit into my costume*?" Kit asked.

"Hard to say," said Angela, never taking her mischievous eyes off me.

I'd known Kit for years, but I thought she'd *always* been like this: confident, dynamic, strong. To be in S.E.C.R.E.T., she must have gone through a time of great fear and self-doubt. Yet she showed no sign of that now. Then there was Angela, a stunning example of physical perfection if there ever was one. Yet knowing what I knew about S.E.C.R.E.T

S . E . C . R . E . T .

and how they pick participants, why was I still so surprised to find that when the pink boa slipped off her arms, Angela was wearing a bracelet too?

"All righty, then," said Angela, extending her hand to help me up from where I was crouched next to Kit. "Upstairs with you, missy. We have some new steps to learn."

"But . . . your bracelets? Are you two—?"

"There'll be lots of time for questions later. Now we dance!" she said, snapping her fingers like a flamenco dancer.

"Speaking of which, where's *your* bracelet?" Kit asked, brushing the dirt off her skin. She was still in her strapless bra and underwear, causing a few stray pedestrians to stop and peer into the front window of Café Rose.

"In my purse," I said.

"Well, that's the first thing you're putting on. My costume is second."

I gulped.

Angela turned me around and launched me back upstairs. When she announced to the rest of the girls that I would be taking Kit's place in the Revue, I expected disappointment or impatience. After all, I would bring the quality of the choreography to a grinding halt. Instead they all clapped and whistled, and positioned me in a line, then helpfully and slowly modeled the first few steps of the routine. Kit, her back miraculously healed, became the ad hoc choreographer, snapping and counting in her bra and underwear. It was like the sleepover I had never been invited to, but with lingerie. When I messed up, no one scolded; they all laughed and made me feel like being an amateur would endear me to the crowd regardless of whether I would hinder their performance. Truth was, their generosity, genuine support and encouragement for this terrifying thing I was about to do brought tears to my eyes, which I was careful to stanch lest I smear my six layers of mascara Angela eventually applied. It took away some of the terror. Some.

Two hours later, one spent learning the group's routine and the other spent with Angela helping me come up with my own, I was backstage at the Blue Nile as the crowd of mostly men streamed in and gathered around the tippy tables in front. Between bouts of practicing, and deeply panicking, I got help from one of the girls in applying the final touches, pressing on a fake mole, adjusting my stay-up fishnets. Finally, Angela stood before me, Kit's burlesque outfit, white lace on black, draping from her fingers, the long pink ties trailing to the floor.

"Okay, babe. One leg, then the other," she said, as she shimmied the tight suit over my thighs. "Turn around, I'll lace you up."

I turned, keeping one hand on my churning gut. I watched as the tighter Angela tied the ties, the higher my breasts swelled over the top of the scalloped bodice. That's when Matilda ducked backstage, the sight of her taking the rest of the air out of my lungs. She smiled at Angela and threw open her arms.

"You're a champ, Angela!" she said, leaning in to whisper to her, "I think you're almost ready to guide. Leave us alone for a bit, my dear."

Angela left, beaming. So she would be a S.E.C.R.E.T. guide soon. I wondered what that felt like.

"Cassie, look at you!" said Matilda.

"I feel like a sausage. I'm not sure this is such a good idea."

"Nonsense." Matilda tugged me completely out of earshot of the other girls to give me some last-minute instructions.

"Tonight, you'll have your pick, Cassie."

"Pick of what?"

"Of men."

"Which men?"

"Men from your fantasies. The ones you've thought the most about over this past year. The ones who've vexed you, and who've left you with lingering thoughts of them. Those men."

"Who? Which ones? *They're here?*" I almost yelled.

Matilda clapped a hand over my mouth. The cold dread pooling in my gut was quickly replaced by nausea.

She gave me a look. "Well, obviously you know who one of them is."

"Pierre?"

My heart leapt at his name. Matilda nodded, a little too somberly, I thought.

"Who else?"

"Who else had you swooning?"

I flashed back to tattooed flesh, a white tank top lifted to expose a rippled stomach . . . the way he laid me across that metal table . . . I closed my eyes and swallowed.

"Jesse."

I was sure I'd never see either of them again, hence my ability to behave with such abandon. Knowing they'd be in the audience, I was certain I'd freeze.

"But do Pierre and Jesse know about each other? And am I supposed to pick one of them and reject the other? I don't know if I'm comfortable with this, Matilda. In fact, I *know* I'm not. I can't go through with this. I can't."

"Listen to me. They don't know about each other. All they know is they've been invited to a legendary burlesque show along with the rest of the community. They have no idea you're performing. And they won't know it's you onstage."

"How are they *not* going to know it's me?"

She reached into her purse and pulled out a Veronica Lake–style platinum blond wig. She spun it around on her fist.

"First, you're going to be wearing this," she said. Reaching back into the bag, she added, "And one of these." She pulled out a sleek, black cat's-eye Mardi Gras mask.

"Remember, Cassie. You're playing a part," she said, speaking slowly and deliberately while expertly fastening the wig over my hair. "You can be nervous up there. The old Cassie might have thought she's not worthy of the attention, or that she's not beautiful or sexy enough to pull it off. But the woman wearing this wig and this mask would never think that. And the men watching her would never believe it. Because she knows not only that she can captivate a man, but also that she's got the whole room in the palm of her hand. There," she said, carefully placing the mask over my eyes and stretching the elastic around the back of my head and releasing it.

"Gorgeous. Now, go be this woman!"

What woman was she talking about? I wondered—until moments later I smacked into her in the backstage mirror.

The girls were gathered in front of it, making last-minute adjustments to their costumes, hair and makeup. I stood among them, equal to them, I thought, no better or worse, just someone taking joy in my body. Just then, Steamboat Betty muscled her way to the front of the pack to aggressively adjust her breasts in her bodice.

"The girls are restless tonight," she said, probably not referring to Les Filles de Frenchmen.

Kit and Angela beamed at me like proud mothers. Then they raised their braceleted wrists at me and gave them a shake. I shook my charms back at them, the collective tinkling like music to my ears.

The band started up. I could hear the MC announce this year's Les Filles de Frenchmen Revue, reminding the men to "give generously" but to "behave respectfully or you're out on your ass."

Angela yelled, "Hurry, Cassie, we're on!"

I took one last deep breath and looked around at my fellow performers, all of us beautiful in our own way, with our wigs and moles and falsies. Each of us was playing a version of ourselves, an exaggerated, alternative and riskier version. Maybe that's what all women do, from time to time. Beneath our everyday costumes, we're all filled with the same fears and anxieties. Angela must have them, and Kit too. But looking at them now, I couldn't picture them hesitating at the red door of the coach house, frozen in fear. The feeling flooding my heart at this moment was gratitude, and some hope that if they were able to step through their fears, I could do it too. I just had to believe I could.

I took my first steps. I found the tempo, counting out the beats audibly, until the line forward-kicked in unison out of the wings and onto the stage, shaking our gloved hands like Fosse dancers. The crowd, darkened behind the bright floodlights, went crazy, which injected us with a kind of performance adrenaline that transferred from one girl to the next, hitting me full force.

"See?" whispered Angela. "I told you they'd love you!"

The first few minutes of the dance were a blur as I adjusted my eyes to the lights and continued to remind myself that no one knew it was me, mousy Cassie from Café Rose. We broke off in our dance pairings onstage, my disguise making it easier to turn my back to the crowd and slowly bump back and forth, following Angela's lead, as the snare drum beat in time to our choreographed gyrations. She was my partner and it was so thrilling to be boldly in tune with the raunchy music and the beautiful Angela Rejean that I began to relax into my body and improvise a little. At one point I was shaking my butt so fast it caused

Angela to throw her head back and let out a whoop. When Angela turned and pranced off the stage right into the crowd, I followed her without thinking, mimicking the way she'd grab a tie and fling it behind a man's head, or mess up his hair, and maybe his wife's too. The women in the audience were having as much fun as the men, our exuberance inspiring them to stand and deliver their own shimmy to the enthusiastic crowd. Some of them were tourists, lucky to stumble upon this local celebration. But I recognized a lot of Café regulars, the musicians, shopkeepers and eccentrics out to cheer on this little pocket of beauty in our bruised and troubled city.

Angela and I performed our choreographed kick-step for the crowd. Then she winked and whispered, "Go along with me, Cass," before she spun, tossed her pink boa around my neck and yanked me into a full-on kiss.

An explosion of clapping and yelling followed as Angela's mouth lingered on mine, and then she finished the kiss with a flourish, nudging me back to my own space. My knees quivering, I tried to continue my choreographed two-step, showing off the garters high on my thighs, but her kiss had thrown me off, bringing the crazed crowd to their feet. I spotted Kit and Matilda sitting together near the bar, clapping and whistling like proud dance moms.

When I turned to blow a kiss to the audience, my eyes rested on a familiar gaze. It was Jesse, occupying a prime table near the front, with a grin on his face that would melt an iceberg.

"Well, hello," he said, leaning back into the chair, taking in the full length of me with a tilt of his head.

How had I forgotten how sexy this man was? This time he wore a snug plaid shirt and jeans, a white undershirt peeking underneath. *That undershirt. His lean concave stomach, his casual hand resting on the hair that leads to . . .* "Oh my God," I said, standing in front of his table. His confused expression reminded me he didn't know who was beneath the wig and mask. I glanced nervously around the room. All eyes were on us. I smiled at Jesse again and froze. Angela took my arm and turned me around for our dual butt-shimmy move. I glanced over my shoulder at him. He was clearly thrilled to be on the edge of the spotlight, a front-row spectator. When we'd finished our little number, he and everyone else in the room erupted into hoots and hollers.

Emboldened by my anonymity, I turned around and leaned forward, placing both hands on his shoulders, and giving him a good long look at the impressive cleavage my dress had enhanced. To any onlooker, it would have seemed we knew each other and were exchanging pleasantries, but when I leaned in, I whispered, "The things I'd like to do to you."

"Whoa, right back at you, baby," he whispered, his hot breath in my ear.

So this is how it works, I thought, taking a finger and placing it under Jesse's stubbled chin. When I brought his eyes to meet mine, I thought I saw a flash of recognition cross his face. I pulled away quickly, and he threw his head back, laughing, loving the flirty attention. Who was this bold woman doing these bold things? This wasn't me. But it was me! And Jesse had had a hand in liberating me.

By this point, all the girls had made their way down from the stage and were working the crowd into a frenzy. Two were now hovering directly over Jesse, who had an expression of pained pleasure on his gorgeous face. Suddenly the girl with the corkscrew curls threw her boa around his neck. I watched her tug him to his feet. While the crowd screamed, he willingly trailed behind her and out the door, the whole time wearing the grin of the luckiest guy in the room. I had had my chance and I hadn't picked him. I smiled and said a silent, wistful goodbye to my lovely intruder.

I followed my duet partner, Angela, farther into the audience. When she moved behind a wide post, I lost sight of her, and moments later locked eyes with another ardent audience member, Pierre Castille, who was leaning cross-armed against the wall, regarding me with a bemused expression, his bodyguard next to him. Here was my choice. *What power you have when you're fully in command of your own body,* I thought. With my hands on my hips, my chin lowered and my shoulders thrust forward, I strutted towards Pierre in rhythm with the drummer's beat. I closed the distance between us, reminding myself I was the girl in the platinum wig and black mask. I could see his Adam's apple bob. At three feet away, I placed a gloved finger between my teeth and pulled off my glove with one tug. I tossed it over my shoulder as the crowd behind me erupted. Then I pulled off the other glove, this time spinning it in my hand. Inches from Pierre, who was now grinning, I reached out and gently slapped him with it, once, twice.

"I hear you're a bad, bad boy," I whispered, in that same breathy voice I had used on Jesse.

"You heard right," he said. He hungrily took me in and then reached out for my waist, as though I belonged to him. As my Prince Charming, when he had claimed me it was part of the role, the fantasy. But his grasp now felt brutish, unkind.

Angela stepped in and scolded him. "Ah, ah, ah. She's not yours, mister. Remember that."

All eyes were on me, even though the other girls had reassembled in a line and were tapping out a goofy number on their way back to the stage. I broke the spell by turning around. With my back to Pierre, I did a little burlesque wiggle, curling my body like smoke in front of him for the edification of the audience. Finally, the spotlight moved away from us and back to the action onstage, giving Pierre the opportunity to gather the strings of my bodice as though he had me on a leash. With a yank, he tugged me backwards to him, his mouth hovering at my ear.

"I thought I'd never see you again, Cassie."

My eyes shot open behind my mask. "How——?"

"Your bracelet. I recognized my charm."

"You mean *my* charm," I said.

"I like you better as a brunette," he said.

I turned around quickly. My breasts brushed his chest. My heels put us almost eye to eye. I felt a sexy toughness swell inside me.

"Well, I liked *you* better as Prince Charming," I said. I might have been wearing a mask, but I could finally see beneath his. While mine hid a few common fears and insecurities, below his surface I sensed menace; women served a purpose, and when he was done with them, he would discard them. He was lovely for a fantasy night, but beyond that, I couldn't imagine a life at his side.

"I'm not yours," I whispered. "If anything, it's the other way around."

Just as the spotlight found us again, Pierre reached a hand to my cleavage and tugged it open. He dropped dozens of gold coins down the front of my bodice, letting a few tinkle to the floor for effect. It shocked me and left me feeling icy cold. The crowd seemed unsure whether to clap or to boo Pierre. The spotlight turned to the stage again, where the ladies were doing their high-kick finale.

"Let go of her," said a voice in the dark. "Or I'll kick you hard in the teeth."

I saw a figure approaching, silhouetted by the lights. But I didn't need some man coming to my rescue. I jerked my bodice out of Pierre's grasp and smacked backwards into Will Foret, who placed a warm hand on my waist to steady me.

"You okay?" he asked.

"Yeah. I'm fine," I said. The snare drums were drawing the finale number to a close.

Will turned to Pierre, who was still leaning arrogantly against the wall. "This isn't a strip club, Pierre."

"I was just rewarding this beautiful dancer with the proper currency," Pierre responded, his hands raised in surrender.

"You grabbed her dress. That's not allowed."

"I didn't know there were *rules*, Will."

"That's always been your problem, Pierre."

Applause broke out in full now, and everyone around us took to their feet in a standing ovation for the girls onstage.

Pierre brushed one sleeve and then the other, straightened his jacket, then offered me his arm.

"This is over, clearly. Let's get out of here, Cassie."

At the sound of my name, Will turned to me, his mouth open. I couldn't tell if he was impressed or disappointed.

"Cassie?"

I pulled off my mask.

"Hi," I said, hands on my bodice. "What can I say? Last-minute replacement."

Will stammered, "I—I thought— I . . . Holy shit. You look incredible."

Pierre's patience was wearing thin. "Can we go now?"

"Yes," I said. But at that moment, I saw Will's shoulders drop, the same way they had at the Ball after Pierre scored the winning bid. Turning to Pierre, I added, "You can go. Anytime."

I took a tentative step towards Will to punctuate the fact that I was making my choice.

"It's you," I whispered. "I pick you."

I watched Will's expression soften into a relaxed victory, made complete when he slid his hand into mine and squeezed it, a gesture so intimate it made me feel faint. Will wasn't taking his eyes off mine. Winning became him, I decided.

Pierre laughed and shook his head, as though Will had greatly misunderstood something important.

"Nice guys do finish last," Will said, looking only at me.

"Who said we were finished?" Pierre replied.

After a lingering look at me, and a cocky smile, Pierre disappeared into the crowd, his bodyguard trying to keep up with him. I was glad to see him go.

"Let's get the hell out of here," Will said, pulling me through the crowd.

As we passed Matilda and Kit's table, they both shook their wrists at me. I shook back. Then I spotted Angela, prancing back to the stage. She, too, turned and gave me a shake, her charms dazzling in the spotlight.

"Hey, she has the same bracelet as you," Will said.

"She does."

A hand reached for my arm. It was that of a squat, middle-aged woman wearing an oversize *They Do Everything Better in New Orleans* T-shirt. "Where can I buy a bracelet like that?" she asked, or rather, demanded. Her accent was New England; Massachusetts or Maine.

"It's a gift from a friend," I said. But before I could pull my wrist away, she had one of my charms pinched between her thumb and forefinger.

"I've got to have one!" she screeched.

"You can't buy it!" I said, easing my wrist out of her grasp. "You have to earn it."

Will pried me away from her and led me past the clog of spectators still at the door. Outside in the brisk winter's night, he threw his coat around my bare shoulders, then pressed my back against the window of Three Muses, unable to wait any longer to kiss me. And kiss me he did. He kissed me deeply, wholeheartedly, stopping every once in a while as if to see if it was actually me who stood in front of him shivering in his embrace. I wasn't cold. I was waking up, my body shuddering to life in his arms. It is one thing to be gazed upon by a man you desire, quite another by one you love. But—I had to ask, even though I wasn't sure I wanted to know the answer.

"Will . . . about you and Tracina . . . ?"

"It's over. It's been over for a while. It's you and me, Cassie. It should always have been you and me."

We let some tourists pass while I took in this heart-stopping information. *You and me.* We walked a few steps farther and Will stopped me again, this time pressing me up against the redbrick wall of The Praline Connection, where a couple of the wait staff inside raised their eyebrows. *Will Foret and Cassie Robichaud?* they must have been thinking. *Kissing? On Frenchmen?*

Will's hands, his smell, his mouth, the love I thought I saw in his eyes, all made such sense. I wanted him, all of him. He was already in my head and heart and now my body wanted him too. When he stopped me in the street again and held my head in his warm hands, searching my eyes for an answer to his unspoken question, I knew he heard my wordless *yes.* We practically sprinted the remaining half-block back to

Café Rose, where Will's hands shook so much he couldn't unlock the door without dropping the keys, twice.

How was it possible he was more nervous than me? How come I wasn't nervous at all?

The Steps.

They cascaded in my mind. I could surrender, finally, to this man I had resisted from the beginning. I felt fearless, brave, generous and confident enough to accept him. I trusted Will, which gave me courage to face whatever our future held. And I was so wildly curious to find out what this man was like in bed, what we would be like together. A new feeling rose inside me, exuberance, the ultimate promise of Step Nine. We were joy in action.

We stumbled into the restaurant, laughing and kissing, tripping over the shoes we kicked off in our rush up the stairs, Will frantically untying the back of my bodice, me helping him off with his T-shirt, in a room that would never feel lonely again.

He was far from the timid lover I had imagined him to be. He was ferocious and gentle all at once, and I reached to match him. I pulled him, kissing him with full force, leaving no mistake about my longing. This man was mine. Standing above me, shirtless, his beautiful arms and chest on display, he whipped off his belt. Then he threw his jeans and underwear across the room.

"Shit," he muttered, something dawning on him. He bolted to retrieve the tossed jeans, shaking them to release a wallet, which he then savaged for a condom. A man had never secured one so fast in his life, I thought, watching him slide it on. Returning to the mattress, he knelt and opened my legs. His eyes took in the length of me, and he shook his head as though he could not have imagined the moment more perfectly. Then he hovered over me, showering me with kisses, gentle, then more deliberate, beginning an achingly slow trail from my neck, down to my clavicle, and lingering at my breasts. I couldn't contain my giggles as he inched his way down me, his stubble tickling my skin. He stopped every once in a while to gaze back up at my face, his eyes searching mine, making me beg for him. *I am about to have sex with Will Foret, my boss, my friend, my man.*

My breathing turned shallow and my back arched as he glided into me. What is it called when you yearn for someone and yet they're right there with you, giving you exactly what you want? What do you call something that stirs your heart, head and body at the same time? With the other men, I had been fully there physically, but my heart was never fully awakened. With Will, every part of me was alive beneath him. My head was saying yes, my body was saying now, and my heart was near to bursting with the wonder of it all. *Is that what it is to love? Yes,* I thought, *this is love.,* I realized. *Here is my love, my young old man, my Will.*

"You're so beautiful like this," he whispered, the words catching in his throat a little.

"Oh, Will." It was hard to believe this was possible, this feeling of ecstasy. I writhed beneath him, mad with desire.

I wanted to come, I had to, and yet I wanted to stop, to freeze this feeling of liquid joy inside of me.

"I've wanted to do this since the day we met," he said.

He moved up to kiss my face. His slow, deep movements elicited a thousand surrenders from me. His elbows rested on either side of my head, as he smoothed back my hair, his eyes searching my face. And then he began to hunger for something he had only begun to taste. I could see it in his expression. In a single smooth motion, he flipped me on top of him.

I placed my hands on his muscled shoulders and my hips matched his rhythm. He was feeling it too, I knew it: a pleasure bigger and stronger than anything experienced before. As bliss shot up and through me, I could only throw myself into it more fervently. When I came, I heard him calling my name, his torso arching as he filled me, melding his beautiful body with mine.

Afterwards, I lay across his chest. The chill outside, our breath, our bodies warming the room had caused the windows to steam up. Before I could really calm my breathing, his mouth found mine for a lingering kiss. Then he fell back again and closed his eyes. Both of us were lost in a quiet serenity.

"I think you're probably going to be late for work tomorrow," he said softly a while later. "And I think I'm okay with that."

I laughed as I rested my head against his chest, listened to his heart. He wrapped his arms around me, pulling me to him, kissing the top of my head.

"Have you really thought of doing that since the day we met?" I asked.

"Yup. And pretty much nothing else, Cassie."

A terrible doubt rose in me. I needed to know.

"So, why did you guys break up?" This explained Tracina's moodiness, her absences the past few weeks.

He closed his eyes like a man who knows he has to deliver news he'd rather forget about. "Couple weeks ago I caught some texts that went back and forth between her and that D.A. from the auction. But it's been over between us for longer. She just handed me an excuse."

"Was she cheating on you?"

"She says no. But I don't really care either way. It doesn't matter. It's over."

"What'll she say when she finds out about us?"

"She'll say, 'Told you so.' She always knew I was a little bit in love with you."

A little bit in love with me? He must have sensed my astonishment. "Yeah, you heard me," he said, tickling my sides. "Does that scare you? Me saying it?"

"Nah, you said *a little bit* in love, you didn't say *a lot* in love. *That* would scare me."

"Well—" he began.

I slapped a hand over his delicious mouth.

"Don't!" I said, resting on an elbow and hovering over his very handsome and now very pensive face.

He removed my hand and kissed it. "You're different than I thought you'd be, you know," he said, regarding me intently.

"You mean . . . in bed?"

"No. I don't mean the sex, not exactly. I mean *you*. You seem more . . . together. More confident, I don't know. I mean, I always saw you like that, but I didn't think you did, until lately. Lately you've just been more . . . more *you*."

I smiled down at him, having just received the best compliment of my life.

"You know, I think you're right. I think maybe I *am* more me lately," I said, leaning in for another kiss.

And moments later we fell asleep to the sound of the sax player who held court after hours in the doorway of Café Rose, hat at his feet, putting his own loneliness to music as mine dissipated into the night.

p

How I left Will sleeping there I'll never know. I guess I assumed I'd see him again a few hours later, after I raced home, fed the cat, showered and put on a nice pair of jeans and a sexy top to open the restaurant.

Turned out I wasn't late. I was early, in fact, early enough that I managed to have the coffee brewed before our first customer walked through the door, stepping over the *Times-Picayune* instead of doing the polite thing by bringing it in for me. But I wasn't mad. Nothing could get me down that day, I decided, not the rain, nor the fact that the girls had left the room upstairs a bloody mess, one that would likely fall to me to clean. After all, Will and I had contributed to the mess, hadn't we? Will and me. Me and Will. Were we an us? I hoped so. *No. It's too soon to think that way, Cassie.* There was still the matter of collecting my charm, and telling Matilda I'd made my decision. I was choosing a relationship with a man I loved over S.E.C.R.E.T. And I was grateful, so very grateful, that this decision was such an easy one to make. The sexual emancipation of Cassie Robichaud was complete.

Admittedly, a part of me would miss the excitement. And I loved the feeling of sorority I got from the women in S.E.C.R.E.T., women like Matilda and Angela and Kit. I could only imagine what it would be like to help facilitate fantasies for another woman, to pass the lessons down. But I wanted a life with Will. Something in me knew it would be fulfilling and loving and fun. He'd already proven to me that sex with him could be all that I needed, wanted or ever imagined. And I was ready to do that for him too.

No, nothing could bring me down on that day, until I saw Tracina trudge around the corner from the condo, waiting for a soda truck to pass before slowly crossing Frenchmen, her arms tightly wrapped around her. I felt a twinge of guilt despite my certainty that I'd done nothing wrong. They broke up. We weren't friends. I owed her nothing. Still, I fled to the back of the Café and busied myself with sandwich prep. My stomach dropped when I heard the door chimes announce her arrival. She said hello to a couple regulars. Why was she here so early? I quickly tossed out a dozen bread slices like I was dealing cards.

"Hey," she said, sending me to the ceiling.

"Ah!"

"Whoa, Cassie, relax. I didn't mean to scare you."

I let out a nervous laugh. "It's okay. I'm just a little jumpy."

She asked about the show. She'd heard that I danced after all.

"I made an ass out of myself," I said, shrugging.

"That's not what I heard."

She knew something. I could tell by the tone of her voice. Will and I had left Blue Nile holding hands.

"I'm just glad it's over," I said, slashing mayo across the bread, avoiding her eyes.

"Did Will show up?"

"Ah . . . I think so, yeah."

"He didn't come home last night," she said, pulling her coat tighter to her. I wanted to scream, *What do you mean, "home"? You guys broke up. He's been sleeping upstairs for the past two weeks! He told me.*

"Did you happen to see him leave last night?"

"I didn't see him leave. Nope," I lied.

"Did you go to Maison with the rest of the girls after the show?"

"Nah, I just went right home."

"I guess that's why I didn't see you there."

My blood chilled. I was being cued that yes, indeed, Tracina knew something. Panic crept in. Would she tear my eyes out, kick in my teeth? Good God, where was Will?

"Will said you weren't feeling well yesterday. Are you better now?" I asked.

"I've recovered. Mornings are the worst. I mean look at my skin," she said. Reluctantly, I scanned her face and had to admit that her skin was a little sallow, her eyes a little sunken. "But the doctor said the morning sickness will pass soon, when I enter my second trimester."

Second trimester? What the——? "Are you . . . ?"

"Pregnant? Yes, Cassie, I am. But I wanted to be sure because I'd been down this road before and then been disappointed. I didn't want to say anything until I knew for certain. And now . . . I know for certain."

She placed a hand on her stomach, which, now that I was staring right at it, did seem to exhibit a bit of a swell.

"Does . . . Will know?"

Her eyes met mine. "He does now. I called him. About an hour ago. He came rushing right over."

It must have been just after I left to go home and change. "What did he say?"

"He was so happy he was . . . nearly in tears. Can you believe that?" she said, her own eyes welling.

I could believe that this news would bring tears to Will's eyes. I could. In fact, right then and there, I also choked up.

"It's all very sudden, I know. But after I told him this morning, he proposed to me. He's such a good man, Cassie. And you know how much he loves my brother. And wants to set a good example for him."

My mind was spinning. *How can this be happening? I picked him and he picked me.*

I opened my mouth, but all I could manage was "I don't know what to say."

She eyed me, her whole body relaxing now that she had this out of her system.

"Just say congratulations, Cassie. Leave it at that."

"Congratulations," I said, moving in for an awkward hug.

I couldn't breathe for a second, so when the doors chimed, I used it as an excuse and quickly walked out front.

But it wasn't a customer. It was Will, looking as haunted as I'd ever seen him.

"Cassie!"

"I gotta go," I said. "Tracina's in the kitchen."

"Cassie, wait! I didn't know! What can I do? What can I say?"

I turned to face him. "Nothing, Will. You've made your choice. There's nothing more to do."

Tears spilled down my cheeks. He reached out to wipe them, but I moved his arm away.

"Please don't go, Cassie," he whispered, begged.

I plucked my coat off the rack and threw it on, leaving the door open as I walked out of Café Rose. As I went south on Frenchmen, the cold rain began to subside. My walk turned to a jog at Decatur as I made my way through the French Quarter, already waking up to the day's festivities. At Canal, Mardi Gras madness was gearing up and I moved through the crowd at a crazed pace. I had to get out of here. At Magazine, when I bent over, gasping to catch my breath, I realized I was still wearing my waitressing apron. I didn't care. Images of my body entwined with Will's flashed through my mind. His kisses, his chest flexing beneath me, the way he cradled my head in his hands. I clutched my side as the sobs wrenched their way to the surface. My Will, my future, dissolved. Just like that. I let a packed bus pass, then another one. I decided to walk to

Third Street so I could keep crying, not caring who saw me, the throngs of tourists fighting for a prime spot on the parade route.

Oh, Will. I loved him, but there was nothing to do. I couldn't be the woman who took a father away from his baby. One perfect night, that's what we had, and now I had to let it go. I'd learned from the other men how to be with them, then let them go. Could I do this with Will? I had to try.

Crossing under the Pontchartrain Expressway, I started to feel my body relax as the tourists thinned out. The dank smell of the French Quarter gave way to the scent of flow-ering vines snaking up the houses in the Lower Garden District. The rain had stopped and the widening sidewalks put my heart at ease.

Turning up Third, I was reminded of my first foray down this lush street and how my fear had stopped me in my tracks so many times that day. Now, I stood here again, soaking wet, my heart bruised. I was once so afraid of the world. And even though I was in pain, the fear was gone, replaced with a true and real sense of myself. I had my feet on the ground. I was heavy-hearted, but I would survive this and be made stronger. I knew what I wanted. I knew what I had to do.

Danica buzzed me past the entrance. I made my way slowly across the courtyard, marveling at how spring came to New Orleans in February. Before I even knocked on the big red door, Matilda opened it, an expectant smile on her face.

"Cassie. Are you here for your final charm?"

"I am."

"So you've made your decision?"

"I have."

"Are you saying goodbye to us, or are you choosing S.E.C.R.E.T?"

I stepped over the threshold and handed Danica my wet coat. "I'm choosing S.E.C.R.E.T."

Matilda clapped her hands, then placed them on my cheeks.

"First let's dry those tears, Cassie. Then we'll phone the Committee. Danica, put some coffee on. It's going to be a long meeting," she said, gently shutting the big red door behind us.

ACKNOWLEDGMENTS

Thank you to everyone at Random House of Canada and Doubleday Canada for throwing instant support behind this book: Brad Martin, Kristin Cochrane, Scott Richardson, Lynn Henry, and Adria Iwasutiak. Also to Suzanne Brandreth and Ron Eckel for your incredible work in Frankfurt. And thank you Molly Stern, Alexis Washam, Catherine Cobain, Jacqueline Smit, and Christy Fletcher for being early adopters. Much gratitude to Lee-Anne McAlear, Vanessa Campion, Cathie James and Charlene Donovan (Monkey!); and for the time off and support, thank you Tracie Tighe, Alex Lane and Mike Armitage. Love and thanks to my family, especially my first reader, my sister, Sue. And if not for Nita Pronovost, my fierce and tireless editor, this book would not exist. Thank you.

READER'S GUIDE TO

S·E·C·R·E·T

ABOUT THE BOOK

Widowed at a young age after a disastrous marriage, Cassie
Robichaud has settled into a quiet life with narrow boundaries: the restaurant where she works, the "Spinster Hotel"
where she lives, and the sad, constant awareness of how long
it has been since she has been with a man. Cassie moves
through her daily routine clad in bleak practicality—hair in a
hasty ponytail, sensible work shoes, stained shirt—escaping
only briefly with a run through her neighborhood, chats with
her boss and friend, Will, and a voyeur's longing for the
romantic happiness that seems to come so easily to her
patrons. When one of them leaves behind a notebook full of
salacious sexual details, Cassie gets her first glimpse into a new
world of sexual empowerment. . . . And her first introduction
to the unusual sorority that will transform her life. Dedicated
to passion, pleasure, and sensual discovery, S.E.C.R.E.T. is all
about women living their sexual lives to the fullest. . . . And
for Cassie, it's the key to sexual emancipation at last.

1. What compelled you to read this book?

2. How does the book fit in with modern popular erotica? Have you read other books with a similarly sexual theme? How does this one compare?

3. Did you enjoy the writing? What constitutes good writing in this genre? Do you hold it to the same standards as other novels or popular fiction?

4. How do you imagine the spark between Will and Cassie first occurred? Why is she so reluctant to date him during the years of their friendship? Do you think they would make a good couple?

5.   What qualities do the members of S.E.C.R.E.T. see in Cassie that make her an appealing candidate? Do you agree with their assessment? Why do you think they are so sure of her acceptance of their offer?

6.   How have Cassie's experiences with her father and husband shaped her view of men and relationships? Does her opinion of men change during the course of the book?

7.   During her ski trip, Cassie reflects on the sacrifices she made for Scott and the ways in which she gave up—or never explored—her own passions in order to please him. Has she begun to more fully explore her own interests through her year with S.E.C.R.E.T.? What is she discovering about herself, and what (if anything) do you think she still needs to discover?

8.   Do you think the "steps" in the S.E.C.R.E.T. process are intended to improve a woman's overall life, or is the focus strictly sexual? How does Cassie's experience with sexual liberation change her outlook on her day-to-day life?

9.   Do you think that organizations like S.E.C.R.E.T. exist in the real world? Would you be surprised to learn of such a group in your town?

10. Cassie begins to recognize the "strange reciprocity" of her S.E.C.R.E.T. encounters. Do you think there is more to the male side of the story of S.E.C.R.E.T.? How do you imagine the recruitment of the men works? What do you think each of the men hopes to gain? Why would each of them have agreed to the arrangement?

11. Who do you imagine the hip-hop star to be?

12. Matilda described the S.E.C.R.E.T. men as "not the greatest life partners." Do you think this quality makes them better candidates for the S.E.C.R.E.T. program?

13. Near the end of her year with S.E.C.R.E.T., Matilda asks Cassie to name her favorite partners. Were you surprised by Cassie's choices? Was there one encounter (or partner) that seemed most interesting or erotic to you? Who would have made your shortlist?

14. On the night of the revue, why do you think Cassie let Jesse go? Do you think she will regret her decision? Would you have made the same choice?

15. At the end of the book, does Tracina know that Cassie and Will spent the night together? Do you think Will actually proposed to Tracina afterward? What do you think will happen to Will and Tracina next?